MR. GLENCANNON IGNORES THE WAR

Collectors' Edition

MR. GLENCANNON
IGNORES THE WAR

This Limited First Edition consists of
nine hundred fifty copies of which this
volume is Number _487_

MR. GLENCANNON IGNORES THE WAR

by

Guy Gilpatric

FIRST EDITION
THE GLENCANNON PRESS
1996

TO
LOUISE

PREFACE

Between 1930 and 1941, several Glencannon
stories a year appeared in the old *Saturday Evening
Post.* They quickly developed a cult audience which
eagerly awaited each subsequent story. Then there
was a dry spell of almost two years. The public
outcry and demand for "more Glencannon" was such
that the *Post* took the unusual step of stating the
fault was not theirs and promised to publish any new
Glencannon story as soon as it arrived.

During the hiatus, Guy Gilpatric wrote other
stories, including *Action In the North Atlantic* which
was made into a movie starring Raymond Massey
and Humphrey Bogart. But, perhaps to appease his
fans, he returned to the pages of the *Post* late in
1943 with *Mr. Glencannon Ignores the War,* his first
book-length work about Mr. Glencannon. It was
worth the wait. The *Post* introduced the story with:
"Long absent and sorely missed, the canny chief

engineer of the *S.S. Inchcliffe Castle* — still vurra fond o' Duggan's Dew — returns to tell what the war did to him. And vice versa!"

As nearly as possible, we have preserved the text of the original story, both as it appeared in installments in *The Saturday Evening Post* December 11, 1943 through January 8, 1944, and by including some text omitted from the magazine serials but found in a volume published by The World Publishing Company in 1945. We are particularly pleased to have obtained permission to reproduce the original *Post* illustrations by George Hughes.

The modern reader may notice how printing styles have changed in the fifty-some years since this story first appeared. For example, we no longer end almost every quote with an exclamation mark. Modern style is to increase the impact of such punctuation by seldom using it. Likewise, the reader will notice a great number of long dashes in the text. The same rule applies in modern writing — greater impact with less usage. Interestingly, however, the earlier style provides a "flavor" that, for those who remember the older series, will evoke the nostalgia of the stories, while creating it for newer readers.

Mr. Glencannon Ignores the War contains one other oddity. It is the only setting in which Guy Gilpatric used fictional place names. This may have been because it was published during wartime and censorship would not allow the use of real locations. Today one can feel fairly confident in reading Pandalang as Singapore. With that as the reference, other directions and locales come into focus.

We hope you find this collectors' edition true to the original, and, perhaps, in some ways, even better. It contains the <u>complete</u> text and the original drawings — a first in book form.

Mr. *Glencannon Ignores the War* is the first volume in our planned series of The Complete Glencannon Stories. Future books will contain reprints of stories grouped around particular themes or subjects. Each volume will be illustrated.

Look for our next in the series, *The Glencannon Menagerie*, some time in 1997. Meanwhile, pull up a chair in front of a crackling fire, pour yourself a glass of Duggan's Dew o' Kirkintilloch, and return to the decks of the *Inchcliffe Castle*. Mr. Glencannon's world is on the verge of changing forever.

Walter W. Jaffee
Editor

FOREWORD

Barnaby Conrad, artist, writer, restaurateur, bull-fighter, and guiding light of a highly-respected West Coast writing workshop, was a close friend of Guy Gilpatric. We wrote asking if he would pen an introduction to our Glencannon series. He replied, "Feel free to use that intro from The Best of Glencannon *. . . I said all I know and feel in it," adding, "I was in Scotland last month and thought of our hero when I ate my first haggis!"*

He writes: "I think what you folks have done — this projected series *— is wonderful, fabulous, heartwarming, and a whole bunch of other adjectives that would have made that modest gentleman, the author, squirm. And, by the bye, I think your opus should be entitled:* Tales of the Most Unmitigated, Scurrilous Rascal Who Ever Lived!"

We think you'll agree Mr. Conrad's delightful piece is as appropriate (and perhaps more poignant) today as it was when he wrote it in 1968. Ed.

"I have an idea for a story," Guy Gilpatric said to me one evening. "A man buys fifty parrots, and taking each one separately he teaches it a singing part. Pretty soon he's got them all trained and he thinks he's got the greatest act show business ever saw. The parrots singing together sound just like the Vienna Choir Boys. Except for one thing. One of the birds — the one with a voice like Pinza — always insists upon singing O'Reilly's Tavern right in the middle of Ave Maria. I haven't figured how it all turns out but it might be worth a whirl."

Guy never got around to working out the end to the story, and it's too bad, for in his hands it would have been a very funny thing. Now the story will never be written and thousands of people the world over will be denied the joy of that rare thing, the hearty, healthy, unfettered belly laugh. He never wrote the story, for on July 6, 1950, he and his beloved wife Louise died tragically in their home at Santa Barbara, California.

It doesn't seem right for tragedy to have had any part of Guy's life, for during it he brought so much laughter to the lives of others. Just a mention of Mister Glencannon and my elderly aunt starts to laugh. My young cousin's rowboat is the Inchcliff Castle, and he is an authority on an incredible variety of skullduggery garnered from a certain walrus-mustached idol of his. I just spoke on the telephone to my wife's uncle and told him I was doing this foreword, whereupon he began to reminisce about his favorite Glencannons and soon he was giggling, spluttering and gagging so that he had to hang up.

This Glencannon disease does not seem to be confined to Americans. Once during the war I was sitting in the lobby of the Hotel Rock in Gibraltar when I saw a civilian in suspiciously deep conversation with two avidly listening British naval officers. I heard snatches of their conversation — "prisoner of the Japanese — disguise — sabotaged the water pumps" — and other bits that made me, as an eager young Vice Consul, think I had stumbled on something BIG. For a brief moment, that is, until the phrase — "a couple of shots of the Dew" floated over to me. I heard the laughter then and realized that here was just a pair of addicts catching up on the latest exploits of their hero.

Their *hero!?*

As a writer I have always been astounded by the phenomenon of the Glencannon stories. Every book on creative writing I've read has agreed that you "must like the main character and be in sympathy with his goal."

What the devil is there to like about Mister Glencannon! Here is an unmitigated, unvarnished, unredeemed scoundrel who in every story dedicates himself to a series of misdeeds which will merely hasten his unswerving path to the heated hereafter. The most charitable person could find absolutely nothing to recommend him. He is canny, aye, that he is, but canniness is not a virtue. He is also a liar, a cheat, a vindictive mercenary blackguard, and an incipient alcoholic. It's better not to go into what would happen if a poor feeble widow happened for some reason to be standing between him and a luscious dollop of Duggan's Dew when the thirst came upon him.

Think of the favorite rogues of fiction — they all have some saving grace, some lovable qualities, no matter how well hidden. Falstaff, Til Eulenspiegel, Robin Hood, Figaro, Candide, Tom Jones, Micawber, Huck Finn, Jimmy Valentine, the Cannery rogues, Hildy Johnson, Sheridan Whiteside, and the Kingfish . . . all of them have redeeming features which make you love them in spite of and because of their faults. Even Mr. Hyde had his good side.

But Glencannon! What can you say in defense of him? The Spanish have a word which suits him to a tee — *sinvergüenza*. It means "incorrigibly without shame." By all rights Colin Glencannon should be the most despised character of all fiction.

But he isn't. He's probably the most widely known and beloved rogue in modern-American fiction, and to heck with the books on creative writing!

It's incredible that such a character could emerge from the personality of Guy Gilpatric, for he was the antithesis of his brainchild. Gentle, warm, honest, generous, modest and painfully shy, perhaps he found refreshing outlets by making his character go to the opposite extreme of these qualities. Guy never liked to talk about Glencannon. He never liked to talk about his work at all, and whenever he did, it was always to laugh at it and dismiss it as being of no consequence to anyone.

He hated talking about himself. He was so modest that I knew him intimately for two years and only knew that he "didn't like airplane travel and always took the train." It was Louise who told me that he was one of the pioneers of American aviation or I never would have known that he'd even been up in a plane, much less held the world's altitude record for several years. He was also a fine fencer, a crack pistol shot, and probably the first exponent of the now popular undersea goggle fishing. He was a voracious reader, and the catholicity of his ideas and interests was highly stimulating to a young and very green writer. I would go up to Guy's two or three times a week, and over a mug or two of Duggan's Dew we would discuss everything under the sun, from spearing robalos in the Mediterranean, to stunting planes for the movies (which he once did also!). And of course, Monty, Monty, his adored dog, killed by a truck, always came into the conversation, and Guy and Louise would grow sad at the memory of their "only child."

Whenever I became stuck on a short story, which was constantly, I would run to Guy. With the greatest of willingness and with no apparent effort he would put his finger on exactly what was wrong with it. Once, by a simple yet ingenious suggestion, he turned a very commonplace story of mine into one which won several awards and is still appearing in anthologies.

Right now I am working on a short story, but I am stuck and I don't know what the trouble is. I wish Guy were here. He would know.

Guy would know for he was a consummate craftsman. He sold his first story to *Colliers* when he was fifteen, and after that he never wrote a story that didn't sell. He wrote a lot of stories too, hundreds of them, and not all about Glencannon. Some — a very few — were serious, but most were calculated to make a person "express mirth by an explosive, inarticulate sound of the voice," (as the dictionary defines laughter). Even though Guy derided his work, constantly apologizing for it because it wasn't "serious stuff," he clearly believed with Rabelais that it is "better to write of laughter than of tears, because to laugh is proper to a man."

"Any darn fool can take a whack at tragedy," William Lyon Phelps once said, "but you have to be touched with genius to write comedy."

Josh Billings said: "Laffing iz the sensation ov pheeling good all over, and showing it principally in one spot."

Now it's time to board the old *Inchcliffe Castle* as she heads out to sea. I, for one, want to be along, because her infamous Chief Engineer gives me the sensation ov pheeling good all over. For Glencannon's gentle and warmhearted creator was touched with the genius that writes great comedy.

Barnaby Conrad
San Francisco
California

1

A long toward sunset, the usual evening breeze fanned out from between the islands and came idling down through Kulong Strait, stirring the kampas trees on the headland, dispelling the smoke haze over the naval dockyard on Victoria Point and filling the sails of the praus and junks which had lain, becalmed and baking, off the Pandalang water front since noon. It was the grateful hour when the city, or at least the Anglo-Saxon portion of it, habitually knocked off from what it was pleased to call its labors, took a shave and a shower, changed into fresh whites, had a couple of short snorts on the home veranda and then drove around to the club for as many tall cool ones as there was time for until dinner. How many in each category it might consume thereafter was a matter which only the individual conscience or capacity could determine; the point was that this pleasant preliminary routine, established by the early colonists and later extolled by Kipling in his ballads of the Empire, had long since transcended the status of mere custom and become a sacred rite. It was simply what one did in Pandalang when the sun hung low and the breeze came idling down through Kulong Strait. No one in Pandalang ever dreamed of doing anything different. Ever, that is, until this evening.

But now that the dream had come, it was a nightmare that everyone was having at once. It followed the familiar panic pattern, in which all the fiends of hell rush gibbering in pursuit, while flight toward an unattainable sanctuary is frustrated by legs turned to tallow and working in reverse on a limit-less dance floor paved with alternate squares of ice and flypaper. There were nearly a million people in Pandalang unanimous in the impulse to go some-where else, and quickly, but they were by no means agreed as to direction. Every boulevard, avenue, street and alley, from stately Governor's Causeway to smelly Hao-kwan Lane, was choked with English, Dutch, Portuguese, Chinese, Hindus, Arabs, Malays and mixtures, in motorcars, busses, rickshaws and ticca-gharris, on horses, ponies, bicycles and on foot; and in each thoroughfare approximately one half of the crowd was headed oppositely to the other. They pushed and kicked and clawed; they howled and cursed in all the tongues of Babel. At a dozen intersections, Sikh policemen were seized by the beard and dragged from their traffic stands, while on the Edward VII Bridge, a detachment of Volunteer Auxiliaries who attempted to straighten things out with their rattan *lathis* were heaved over the parapet into the mud. It was simply a wholesale community funk such as sends anthills into seething dithers and causes herds of cattle to stampede without reason. But Pandalang had a reason. The reason was the Japs.

Two weeks before, when the Imperial Nipponese Third Army crossed the frontier and started down through the jungles and rubber estates of the peninsula, the bilious old curry-fed warriors of Pandalang's club-chair cavalry scowled across their gin *pahits* and swore by gad that the impudent yellow beggars would soon catch a thrashing they'd jolly well remember. When Sindalam Province fell, they said, haw, yes, quite so — the stupid little swine had blundered into a trap where our chaps would literally mow them down and hack them to pieces. The news of Malican's fall they took in ominous silence with the morning dose of liver salts. The surrender of Kohlur next day, however (it yielded without firing a shot) spurred them to drastic action. Unsheathing their fountain pens, they wrote sizzling letters to the *Pandalang Advertiser* and the *Straits Planter's Mail*, asserting that things had come to a pretty pass and demanding that the brass-hatted dunderheads responsible be booted out of the service and flogged to within an inch of their lives in Lord Wellesley Square. But now that two Japanese mechanized divisions were clattering hell-bent down the Grand Peninsular Highway a scant ten miles from the city, these bellicose gentry sat sweating in the traffic jam, sounding their motor horns, bawling at the natives and vaguely wondering if the sun, which had just sunk into the blood-red waters of Kulong Strait, had not at last flouted tradition and set on the British flag. Yes, blast it all, and right at drink time, too!

Perhaps the wildest of all the excitement prevailed on the Bund, a broad, palm-lined esplanade extending along the eastern water front. Here, with a roar of escaping steam, the booming blasts of whistles and the slow thrash of propellers, ships loaded with refugees were casting off their lines and backing out into the dusk, followed by wails and imprecations from the thousands left behind. By eight o'clock but one vessel remained — the S.S. *Inchcliffe Castle*, of London. She was an ancient Clyde-built tramp of some 3500 tons, so decrepit that only the rust and her degaussing belt held her together. In her dingy black war paint streaked with the salt rime of the seven seas, she looked like a boozy old lady who had sullied her widow's weeds by inadvertent contact with too many whitewashed walls. Though the plume of steam which wavered above her funnel indicated her preparedness to put to sea, she showed no signs of doing so. On the quay alongside, a polyglot mob was clamoring to get aboard, but her ladder had been hoisted safely out of reach and, to discourage aspiring hawser climbers, a rather more-than-life-size bos'n was patrolling the decks, an Enfield rifle cradled in the crook of his arm.

Up on the *Inchcliffe Castle*'s bridge, screened from the vulgar gaze by the dodger and the awning, three of her officers were sitting in canvas deck chairs, listening to the tumult and cursing the heat and the state of the world in general. Captain Ball, an elderly mariner of considerable girth, was wearing his uniform cap and a Balinese-batik sarong which had slipped its moorings and drifted several degrees south of his umbilicus; Mr. Montgomery, the mate, was garbed in khaki shorts and a sufficiency of hives, while Mr. Colin Glencannon, the chief engineer, wore only a brier pipe, a whisky breath, a walrus mustache and a luxuriant growth of reddish-brown shag. This hirsuteness was particularly dense upon his chest, which resembled the brisket of one of the hairier species of Highland cattle, but there was no portion of his torso which Nature had not clothed at least as modestly as, say, a pedigreed Airedale. Although Captain and Mate were constantly engaged in repelling gnats, mosquitoes, giant-winged cockroaches and other tropical fauna which came zooming out of the night, it was notable that all these creatures gave Mr. Glencannon a wide berth.

From the direction of Victoria Point came the rumbling thunder of bombs and the thud of

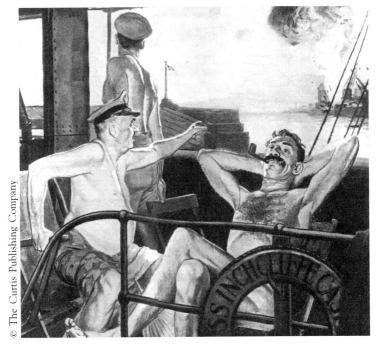

"There! Listen! They're bombing the dockyard!" said Captain Ball.

artillery, evoking an increased clamor from the quayside mob.

"There! Listen! They're bombing the dockyard!" said Captain Ball. "Damn it all, gentlemen, I mean to say, if they don't send us our orders to clear out of here pretty quick, this ship's name won't be *Inchcliffe Castle* but *Itchi-Kitchi Maru*. Ker-hem! Ker-hapf!" His paunch heaved seismically and over the top of his sagging sarong his navel winked like a bleary, cyclopean eye. "I mean to say, I'd take her out this very minute on my own responsibility, only I've got strict orders not to without unloading."

"— So here we sit and twuddle our thumbs while all hell unloads on us!" growled Mr. Glencannon. "Ah, foosh!" he winced. "Just hark to yon thumping and crashing the noo! — See the frichtful flashes reddening the sky! Why, it mak's me sproot oot with goose pimples the size o' mushrooms! — No, fronkly, Captain and Muster Montgomery, I'm not going to foncy wutnessing this war at feerst hond a ha'porth!"

"— Not going to fancy witnessing it at first 'and?" said Mr. Montgomery, challengingly. "'Ow the 'ell 'ave yer been witnessing it, then, ever since it started back in thirty-nine? Didn't yer witness it at first 'and when the torpedo exploded in number two 'old, that time off Cape St. Vincent? Wasn't it bleddy well first 'and when them Stukas bombed and strafed us in the Channel and sunk nine ships out of the convoy? And if you wasn't witnessing the war at first 'and that night we was caught in Lime'ouse Reach during the Big Blitz — well, just exactly wot was you doing with it?"

"I was ignoring it," said Mr. Glencannon. "I was ignoring it utterly. That, I find, is the one and only way to mak' war endurable to my nairves. Fortunately, my duties aboard the ship dinna require my presence on deck, whuch is why ye so seldom see me there. Not being on deck, noturally I canna see the war going on around us in the great ootdoors — indeed, I canna even hear it, because the puir auld rickety engines mak' such a shocking din that they droon oot all exteernal noises short o' a direct hit. Thus, with a certain amoont o' whusky to supply the necessary sunshine vitamins, I can stay doon in the engine room and ignore the war vurra comfortably indeed, thonk ye!"

"Oh, yus? Well, if you've been able to ignore it by staying drunk and down in the engine room until now, why don't you keep on ignoring it by staying drunk and down in the engine room from now on?"

"Sumply because noo the engine room is too dom hot to stay doon in, drunk or sober. Ye see, Muster Mate, we hoppen at this moment to be in the truppics, proctically astraddle o' the Equator; hadn't ye noticed it, ye stupid lout, or did ye think that the prickly heat ye're sporting on yere rump was frostbite?"

"Never you mind what I thought about it," said Mr. Montgomery sullenly, at the same time scratching himself. "Anyway, it ain't prickly 'eat, it's only 'ives, and it's neither 'ere nor there. The point is, now that the Jap army is closing in on one side and their fleet is barging down the strait on the other, you're going to be a first 'and witness of a first-clarss war, whether you like it or not. Only they bottle us up, you'll. . . ."

"Bottle?" Mr. Glencannon started forward in his chair. "Weel, a thousand thanks for reminding me! See here, sir," he turned to Captain Ball, "I just noo realize that I'm doon to my vurra last bottle, and shud we put to sea tonicht, I'll be faced with the grim spectre o' privation. With yere kind permission, I'll just step ashore to the commissary, over yon in Clive Street, and buy mysel' an odequate supply."

"Oh, by all means, yes, yes, go ahead!" said Captain Ball, who had learned through years of experience that alcoholic fuel for the chief engineer was no less essential to the *Inchcliffe Castle*'s operating efficiency than the bituminous variety for her furnaces. "In case our orders come, I'll give you three blasts on the whistle. You'd better rush right back, if you don't want to get left behind!"

"Yus, and you'd better put on some clothes, front and be'ind, if you don't want to add to the panic," grunted Mr. Montgomery.

Mr. Glencannon descended from the bridge and hurried aft to his room, where he donned a clean white uniform and two sets of brass knuckles, one on each fist. These were massive bijoux of his own design and fashioning, with half-inch spikes jutting out at unexpected places.

"They'll save me from fatigue whilst threading my way through the crowds in the blackoot," he murmured. "However," he uncorked his last remaining bottle, "it will be no more than pruddent to fortify mysel' with a wee drap besides. . . ."

Although the knuckle-dusters functioned in a gratifying manner, especially on Portuguese, he was hot and disheveled when he reached the corner of Clive Street and parched with thirst when he had battered his way through the throng which choked the narrow pitch-black mouth of it. A single plane came droning overhead, searchlights probing for it futilely. Somewhere on the Bund a battery of four-point-sevens went crashing into action, and from roof tops all over the city, machine guns spat red tracers into the sky. A shell fragment ricocheted off the house front opposite and whizzed past Mr. Glencannon's left ear, causing the hairs therein to wilt like grasses stricken by a sudden blight. He pressed himself back against the wall and stood cowering. "Great swith!" he panted. "That one was too close to ignore! It's high time I got in from oot o' doors, but it's so dark I canna see whuch door to get into to get oot o' it."

Just then, the lone plane cut loose a parachute flare and the city of dreadful night became one of still more dreadful day. In the clear cold light of that floating magnesium star, a million people knew the paralyzing terror of the rabbit caught in the open when the hawk wheels overhead. Mr. Glencannon shrank three sizes within his clothes; he licked his lips and rolled his eyes aloft. But suddenly he emitted a joyful hoot, for there, a scant six feet above him, he saw what he had been looking for all along. It was a sign which read:

EMANUEL MOOKERJEE & CO., LTD.
Ship Suppliers and Victuallers
Purveyors to H.M.Navy, the P.&O. Steamship Co.
and Other Leading Lines

It was the lower half of the sign, however, which caused his pulse to quicken and his very soul to soar. And no wonder, for it read:

Sole Concessionaires for
DUGGAN'S DEW OF KIRKINTILLOCH
The World-Renowned Scotch Whisky

Mr. Glencannon wrenched open the door, slammed it behind him and stood blinking in the light. From behind the counter at the right came a fat Bengali half-caste wearing a green celluloid eye shade, horn-rimmed spectacles, a black alpaca frock coat and tight pongee breeches. He was shod in heelless slippers which slapped softly as he walked.

"Ho, a vurra guid evening to ye, Muster Mookerjee!" Mr. Glencannon greeted him, raising his voice to make it heard above the din from without. "'Business as usual,' eh, Muster Mook?"

Mr. Mookerjee bowed and smiled unctuously. "Yes, business as usual. Ah, we British!" he said, with the accent known in the East as *chi-chi*, and which sounds as though the speaker had pickled his palate in green persimmon juice. "But this is an honor, Mr. Glencannon! Have a chair, please, and help yourself to a choice, most exceptional cigar, do."

"Thonk ye, I will," said Mr. Glencannon, helping himself to six of them. He broke the end off one, crumbled it into his pipe and lit it. "Fuff

. . . fmaff . . . fmuff . . . not bad!" he announced. "What else are ye giving away, Muster Mook?"

"Eh? Ah, of course!" Mr. Mookerjee said. "Would you care to join me in a little spot of choice, most exceptional whisky?"

"No, I wud not," said Mr. Glencannon austerely. "However, if ye'd care to offer me a respectable mon-size sowp o' it, I'd be hoppy to accommodate ye."

"Eh? Ah, yes, yes, yes!" Mr. Mookerjee placed a bottle of Duggan's and two glasses on the table, then opened a closet containing a refrigerator and brought out ice and soda.

Mr. Glencannon looked askance at these accessories, seized the bottle and helped himself. "A-well, cheerio!" he said, raising his glass politely. "I must say that for a prusperous merchant face to face with ruination, ye're taking things vurra calmly, Muster Mook!"

Mr. Mookerjee shrugged and spread his fat hands. "Ruination? Oh, hardly that!" he said easily.

"Aye, ruination — exockly that! — Stark, staring, stinking ruination — unless ye liquidate yere stock while ye've still got the chonce! Come, let's get doon to business, mon! How much will ye knock off the regular price o' Duggan's by the case? — For spot cash?"

"But why should I knock off anything, my dear Mr. Glencannon?"

"Because ye'll be better off selling it to me for what ye can get than letting the Jops get it for nothing."

Again Mr. Mookerjee shrugged and smiled as he watched his visitor refill his glass. "Really?"

"Aye, dom really!" said Mr. Glencannon, beginning to lose patience. "Oh, it's all vurra canny o' ye to sit there smiling behind yere weel-known unscrutable Oriental mosk, but I'm a shrewd bargainer too! If ye think I'm going to pay ye the regular list price for Duggan's Dew, tonicht, in the face o' a falling market, ye've got another think coming!"

"Ah, indeed? But please to remember, Mr. Glencannon, Duggan's Dew of Kirkintilloch is a superior, most exceptional product — the unvarying choice of discriminating connoisseurs in clubs, bars, private homes and, in fact, wherever an aged, mellowed and truly select Scotch whisky is apprec . . ."

"Aye, I can read the label too!" stormed Mr. Glencannon, tilting his head sideways and doing so while pouring himself another drink. "The point is, what discount will ye allow me, in view o'. . . ."

Whoom!

The premises of Messrs. Emanuel Mookerjee & Co., Ltd., rocked on their foundations.

WHOOM!

The lights went out.

WHOOM!

There was a long-sustained, shivering crash as hundreds of cases and thousands of bottles went tumbling to the floor. Mr. Glencannon dived under the table, but not before a large area of ceiling plaster had shattered on his head. Then the lights came on again and through a fog of dust he saw Mr. Mookerjee on all fours, heading for the cellar. The Bengali's erstwhile liver-colored face was now the shade of putty.

"A-weel, he's shed his unscrutable Oriental mosk, at any rate!" said Mr. Glencannon, emerging from under the table and soothing his jangled nerves with a six-gulp sedative direct from the bottle. "Whoosh, what a wreck! I'll wager the avaricious glaggy is kicking himsel' the noo that he didna listen to reason and accept my cash!"

Feeling a peculiar but not unpleasant tingling sensation in his feet, he looked down and saw that he was standing shoe-deep in a flood of mingled beverages from the world's leading breweries, vineyards and distilleries, and that the tide was still rising. "Ah, war!" he shook his head sadly. "What frichtful waste is wasted in thy name! But at the same time," he wiggled his toes within his shoes, producing a squirping sound, "at the same time, I canna deny that this is a vurra luxurious and de luxe feeling. And — fmff! — the aroma is nothing short o' delichtful!" He stood there, still squirping and sniffing and scanned the shelves to see what stock remained. For some reason, however, his vision was blurred. "Strange!" he mused, "it must be an occular bi-focal refroction, or at least an analogous phenomenon, produrp!, produced by looking through fumes.

The fumes being those o' alcohol, the logical anti-
dote is, o' course, an odequate dose o' some o' the
same."

A sizeable jolt of the same remained in the
bottle, but when he had consumed it, he was dis-
mayed to find his vision even more blurred than
before. It occurred to him, then, that inasmuch as
the causative fumes were emanating from a complex
mixture of liquors, only an approximately similar
mixture could effectively counteract them. Accord-
ingly, he knocked the necks off random bottles of
champagne, brandy, absinthe, slivovitz, arack, gin,
strega, vodka, marc, mirabelle and several others he
was unable to pronounce, and quaffed assiduously.
The results were most gratifying. The blurriness
subsided and not only did his vision become keen as
that of an eagle, which beholdeth all, but he was
actually obliged to squint his eyes in order to avoid
seeing double.

"A-weel," he said, "so much for the medicinal
part o' it; noo to find something to drink!" Squishing
through liquor and crunching on broken glass, he
made his way around the end of the counter. On
the floor behind it he discovered precisely what he
had come for — a full case of Duggan's Dew of
Kirkintilloch. Observing that one of the boards
across the top had been loosened by the fall, he
shook it to make sure that its contents were undam-
aged. Just as he was preparing to depart with his
booty, he happened to notice two more cases lying

unscathed in the corner. "Haw, losh!" he chuckled. "Who shall say there is no bomb in Gilead?"

Through the tumult of the air raid came three hoarse hoots of the *Inchcliffe Castle*'s whistle. Balancing his cases of Duggan's one on top of the other, Mr. Glencannon lurched out into the night.

2

Twenty years of toil and untold millions of money had made of the Royal Naval Dock yard on Victoria Point an establishment unequaled in the Orient and unsurpassed in the world. Within its vast acreage were dry docks, foundries, engine and ordnance repair shops and all else needed to maintain a mighty fighting fleet ten thousand miles from home. It was what the Japanese wanted in Pandalang; they wanted it badly and wanted it intact, which was why they were bombing it so lightly while blasting the everlasting chutney out of the city itself. As a matter of fact, the bombs their Kawanishi 90s and Mitsubishi 96s were dropping on the base were far less annoying than the salvos of conflicting orders which were pouring in upon it from London.

At nine thirty-one came a message, "*Execute Plan K immediately*" — Plan K being a scorched earth demolition by explosives of all installations and matériel likely to be useful to the enemy in the event of capture. Admiral Sir Richard Keith-Frazer, commander of the base, had scarcely finished reading one order when he was handed another; "*Do not execute Plan K except as last resort.*" Within something less than five minutes, this was followed by a third communication: "*Plan K nullified as of this date. New and improved plan for demolition, to be designated Plan K-2, now in formulation by special board. Details will be furnished when available.*"

"Damn!" said Admiral Keith-Frazer, a white-haired and wrinkled but ruddy and spry old gentleman whose northeast corner was completely covered with vari-colored ribbons. He had gone to sea as a midshipman at thirteen years, served upon it with distinction for a full forty-three, and for the past seven had fervently prayed God to send him back there. For these seven years had been devoted to the thankless task of warning the Admiralty that someday there would happen at Pandalang exactly what was happening now. Time and again he had pleaded for more planes and urged the construction of exterior land defenses in depth, pointing out that though the present coastal batteries effectively commanded the Kulong Strait, they could not be brought to bear on landward approaches through an arc of some hundred and eighty degrees — which arc was perilously bisected by the Grand Peninsular Highway. Their lordships in London had merely raised skeptical eyebrows, murmured polite pooh-poohs and agreed among themselves it was a jolly good thing that old Dickey Keith-Frazer was nearing the retirement age. But tonight, the confusion that reigned in Pandalang was having its counterpart at its distant, original source, and as the frantic bureaucrats scurried through the corridors of Whitehall, the ghosts of Gilbert and Sullivan stood chuckling in the shadows, while the ghost of Nelson wept. . . .

A stick of two-hundred pounders crashed down on the Marine Light Infantry Parade Area, and from all over the station the ack-ack cut loose in earsplitting frenzy. An orderly came in from the code room. "Urgent signal from London, sir!" he reported, obliged to shout in order to be heard. The admiral took the message and read: "*Please furnish at once complete data concerning comparative perishability of Brazilian and Venezuelan beverage cocoa as issued for use aboard H.M. ships in tropical waters, giving exact percentages of loss by weight due to evaporation of the butter fat content.*"

"Damn!" said the admiral, who was a man of few words, but with a tendency to repeat himself. For the next quarter hour he was busy at the telephone. When he had hung up, he sat for a moment glowering at a new dispatch which lay before him on his desk. But suddenly, as its meaning bore in upon him, he emitted another "Damn!" — this one an expression of sheerest joy. For — yes, there could be no doubt about it! — the message read: "*You are hereby relieved of command of the Royal Naval Dockyard Establishment at Pandalang and directed to proceed immediately to the fleet at sea, taking command thereof upon your arrival.*"

Admiral Keith-Frazer sprang to his feet, feeling twenty years younger than he had felt twenty seconds before. "Ha! Gad! I've got to get out of here before they change their minds! Captain Campbell!" he roared. Commander Harrod! Curtis! Henshaw! Bigelow! Here, read this, gentlemen, read it! It means I'm off, d'you understand? Off, and out of this bloody mess! Off, to where I can really fight and — and do some good! Well, what are you waiting for? Call my car, somebody — and you, Henshaw, telephone the air station to have a seaplane warmed up and ready!"

"The air station is completely knocked out, sir. The report just came through."

"— Eh, — what? Damn! How am I to get out to the fleet, then? — Swim? — Wade? — Hunh? Speak up, somebody!"

"Well, sir, there still may be that American liaison officer's plane. He left it moored over in the Destroyer Anchorage and. . . ."

"Get him!" barked the admiral. "Get him — and don't decode another blasted Admiralty signal till I've cleared out of here!"

Shortly, a marine orderly escorted a khaki-clad American naval officer into the room. The

American came to attention and saluted. "Commander Barry, United States Navy, Sir," he said.

"Barry? Ah! I need your plane to get me out of here, Commander Barry. Must join the fleet immediately. That pin in the chart marks the position reported at eighteen hundred; course, one-six-seven; speed, sixteen knots. Can we make it?"

"Yes sir."

"Good! Wait for me out in the car." The admiral turned to his officers, gulped once or twice, then smiled. "— Well," he extended both hands in an impulsive, boyish gesture, "good-bye, Campbell! Good-bye, Harrod! Good-bye, all of you! This is your show now, gentlemen. Bad show, too, I'm afraid! Rotten bad! But I'll do what I can to square things at sea, so help me God!"

When he had gone, Captain Campbell shook his head. "He's got to get clear across Pandalang to reach that plane — and the whole town's burning. Then he's got a long, long flight in the dark to get out to the fleet."

"— If he can find it!"

"Yes — and suppose he finds it right in the middle of a full-scale battle!"

"Well," Captain Campbell smiled grimly, "if it isn't in battle when the old boy finds it, it jolly soon will be, once he takes command!"

Now that the city was completely ablaze and their ground forces moving into it from three sides, the Japs ceased their bombing. As Admiral Keith-

Frazer's car alternately crawled through narrow, smoke-filled streets and sped all-out across devastated parks and squares, he and Commander Barry could hear rifle fire even above the crackling roar of flames and the crash of falling walls.

"Damn! They're fighting in the streets!" grunted the admiral. "— Shouldn't be surprised if we had to abandon the car, Barry. Simply cut and run for it, I mean!"

"Looks like it, sir. But if we do — and if we get separated — Lieutenant Gaines is waiting aboard the plane and will fly you wherever you want to go. He's a good pilot, sir!"

"He'll need to be. I say, driver, who are those fellows out there ahead in the road? No, don't stop, don't stop — I don't care if they are waving! Step on it, man!" The smoke-grimed figures scattered as the car plunged through. "British infantry," Barry identified them. "They were shouting something about Japs ahead."

They turned into a street so narrow that at times their tires screeched against both curbs at once. From the windows of the few houses not yet burning came spitting yellow flashes and the dry CRACK! of rifles. Suddenly, fifty yards ahead, the entire front of a three-story building swayed, staggered intact out into the roadway and there collapsed upon itself in a swirling mass of sparks. The driver brought the car to a slithering stop, its wheels bumping over the scattered rubble.

"Blocked, by gad!" said the admiral. "— Out we get!"

In a dark doorway to the right, a lieutenant of infantry appeared. His helmet was dented, his face was bloody and he held, very gingerly, a tommy gun too hot to handle with comfort.

"Well, my pretty dears, thus ends the elopement!" he said cheerily. "— No Gretna Green tonight! And you turtle doves can't get out of here the way you got in, either — they've occupied that building at the corner and . . . Oh! He snapped up stiffly to attention. "Beg pardon, sir!"

"You mean they're at both ends of the street?"

"Yes, sir — and closing in from both directions, sir."

The admiral grimaced and stood biting his lip.

At this tense moment, through the sounds of strife, there came a snatch of song, "My love is lik' a red, red rose," and up the center of the street approached a most peculiar figure. As much of him as could be seen was dressed in the white uniform of the British Mercantile Marine, but a large section of his person was screened from view by three cases of whisky, balanced precariously one on top of another, which he bore before him in his arms. Due to the considerable height of his burden, he was obliged to lean out to one side of it in order to see his way, like a locomotive engineer leaning from his cab. As he walked he teetered, and as he teetered he hic-cuped; that he could still balance his cases and sing

a ballad at the same time was a crowning demonstra-
tion of his virtuosity.

Behind him, around the corner of the street,
a dozen squat figures appeared. They moved furtively, crouching in the shadows of the walls. Without
a word, Commander Barry stepped into the singer's
path and felled him with a right to the jaw. As he
wilted to the pavement the ballad ended on a soul-
piercing note. "Quick, sir!" Barry urged the admiral.
"Peel off your cap and jacket and get into this fellow's
things! Those Japs would give their eyeteeth to
capture an admiral — but even if they do, they
musn't know it!"

Admiral Keith-Frazer hesitated for an instant;
then, "Right! Absolutely!" he agreed, tossing his
own things into the car and hastily putting on Mr.
Glencannon's. He turned to the young man with
the tommy gun. "Lieutenant, you've got to get us
through this house and out the back way. — Quick!"

When Mr. Glencannon regained consciousness and found himself lying in the gutter beside a
large and obviously expensive motorcar, his natural
conclusion was that he had been run over and his
spontaneous impulse was to gouge the owner for
damages. "Oh-oh, see here, noo, ye dom speed
monioc!" he began threateningly, getting to his feet.
"Dinna delude yersel' that ye can get awa' wi' this,
my fine fellow! Will ye settle for ten quid in cauld
cash, here and noo, or must I drog ye into the law
courts and hire wutnesses who will swear ye were
doing seventy miles an hour and had liquor on yere

breath besides? Whoosh, I can even smell the sickening reek o' it from here!" Disappointed at finding the car unoccupied and himself uninjured, he leaned against the fender for support while he endeavored to piece things together. "Noo, let's see, let's see!" he mused. "I was having a vurra enervating time lugging yon cases o' Duggan's through the highways and byways when suddenly all went blonk. No doot I collapsed under the strain, whereupon the owner of this car stopped to give me a lift. But — I wonder what has become o' him?" He peered up and down the street, the houses on both sides of which were now masses of crackling flame. "Losh!" he observed, "a mon wud almost be inclined to say that the town was on fire, if the stoggering cost o' such a thing didna put it oot o' the question! In any event, I canna stond aroond here wasting my time all nicht!" He opened the door of the car and loaded his whisky aboard; then, noticing the white cap and jacket lying on the cushion, he suddenly realized that he was bareheaded and coatless. "Strange!" he muttered. "I dinna remember taking them off, so I'll put them on richt awa' before I forget again."

Mr. Glencannon had driven a car only twelve feet, seven inches in his life, and then off the end of a dock, but he prided himself on his ability in all fields of mechanical endeavor, and so did not hesitate to climb in and step on the starter. Simultaneously, a crackling fusillade of rifle shots rent the air. "Tsk, tsk! She's backfiring because she's a wee bit cauld," he said. "What this car needs is a guid, fast workoot!" He slipped into gear, bore down on the accelerator and got off to a spectacular start. "Dom!" he nodded approvingly. "She's got a lithe, lively pickup — a wealth o' smooth-flowing power — a friendly, eager responsiveness in city troffic or on open highway, which mak' it the unvarying choice o' discriminating connoisseurs in clubs, bars, private homes and in fact wherever an aged, mellowed and truly select automobile is appreciated." He settled down under the wheel and was preparing to enjoy the ride when he happened to notice that he was traveling backwards. For a moment this was disconcerting, but after proceeding stern first for a block or two he realized that as long as he was not driving in a race and had no idea where he was going anyway, whichever of the two ends of the vehicle arrived there in the lead was a matter of purely academic consequence. Luckily, the curbs of the narrow thoroughfare tended to hold the car on its course, and though from time to time it jumped the track and went scraping along the house fronts for considerable distances, it always dropped back into the groove.

A burst of tracer bullets came streaking after him, leaping and spattering off the cobblestones like a swarm of red-hot wasps. "Haw! Fireworks! Oh, how lovely!" he applauded the display. "This, o' course, is the famous and picturesque auld Chinese quarter, or whatever it is, and our celestial brethren are all oot in the streets ceelebrating their annual yearly ceelebration o' the New Year. Aye, a vurra

hoppy New Year to ye, one and all! Haw, haw, haw
— weel thonk ye, Glencannon, and a vurra hoppy
New Year yersel'! The same to you and many o'
them, Colin, dear chum! And look — look yon,
everybody! — Why, be dom if here isn't auld Colin
Glencannon stoggering in on us to bid us Hoppy
New Year! Come on, noo, everybody — let's give
him a cheer! Bottoms urp, Glencannon — ye're a
prince o' guid fellows and two o' nature's noblemen!"

Up the street from the opposite direction,
and unperceived by Mr. Glencannon in his swoop-
ing, backward flight, came a long line of Japanese
tanks, like a herd of elephants lumbering through a
jungle fire. They were coming in a hurry, cutouts
open, motors roaring and treads a-clatter on the
cobblestones. The driver of the leading tank, peering through his slit in the armor, was horrified to
discern a large black motorcar bearing down upon
him in reverse, apparently out of control. He sounded
his horn, slammed on his brakes, gritted his teeth
and closed his eyes. There was a mighty, rending
crash as the car struck the tank and climbed halfway
up the front of it, where it hung drooping like a
punctured accordion.

With an oath, Mr. Glencannon flung open
what was left of the door, leaped out and strode
around to the rear to admonish whoever was
responsible for the outrage. Still half stunned, the
tank driver thrust his helmeted head through the
hatch and blinked his slant eyes through his goggles.
"Hey, what the hell is?" he demanded shrilly, in his

grogginess mentally transported to Ventura, California, and the seat of his old Chevy vegetable truck. "This one-way street, you back up, no stick out hand, all smash, I sue!"

"Oh, aye?" Mr. Glencannon stepped up close and protruded his jaw belligerently. "Weel, noo, just hold on a minute, laddie — tak' it easy and keep yere shirt on! In the feerst place, if ye'll look at that license plate whuch is crumpled up there richt under yer chin, ye'll see ye've smoshed into an official car, so foosh to yere one-way street! In the second place, ye're the second speed-crazy road hog to involve me in as many serious occidents in half as many minutes and I'm getting sick o' it. In the theerd place, ye're nowt but a nosty little yellow-bellied fud, and if ye'll step oot o' that junk heap for a minute, I'll smoosh yere oogly yowp for ye!"

All down the stalled column, the drivers were sounding their horns, flashing their headlights, racing their motors and chatteringly protesting the delay. It was like a traffic jam in Piccadilly. The major in command, who had chivalrously relinquished the honor of leading the column through the town to a junior officer who had not yet heard about land mines, came hurrying up from somewhere in the rear, cursing sibilantly. As he waddled along in his bulky canvas overalls, he looked like an infuriated gnome. As soon as he spied Mr. Glencannon, however, a surprising change came over him. He drew in his breath, saluted and bowed three times from the waist. At the lowest point in the third bow, a brass-knuckled fist whizzed past his chin, missing it by the scantiest of margins. With obvious regret but commendable dexterity, he jerked out his automatic and whacked Mr. Glencannon over the head with it.

"Corporal Sato, search the wrecked car," the major ordered. "Transfer everything that you find in it to Tank Number Twenty. Sergeant Yamura, you will have this prisoner carried back and put in with me. Treat him very gently and with the utmost respect!"

3

Mr. Glencannon was recalled to a state half-way between somnolence and consciousness by the sounds of a distant bombardment. He lay with his eyes closed, listening to it. He had no idea where he was or how he had come there. He suspected that he was in serious trouble and that the war was mixed up in it somehow, but he refrained from trying to recall its exact nature, lest the truth, suddenly flooding in upon him, should prove as devastating as he feared. Besides, he was resolved to adhere to his established policy of ignoring the war and all its ignoble works. "No — I willna even dignify the war by thinking aboot it!" he promised himself. "I shall continue to ignore it, boycott it and shun it till I've won it, and from then on, to hell with it!"

The bombardment increased in intensity and seemed to be coming nearer. He emitted a long-drawn "WHOOSH!" which agitated the bristles of his walrus mustache like thatch on a cottage in the storm-swept Hebrides. While endeavoring to read-just his mouth after this gusty outgiving, he became aware of a very considerable discomfort within it; indeed, his oral cavity felt as though it were occu-pied to capacity by an object which, from its size, shape, texture and taste, he concluded could only be one of his own shoes. This conclusion, reassuring in so far as it identified the shoe as his own and not one belonging to say, the ship's cook, a Norwegian coal passer or Mr. Montgomery, still did not explain how it had happened to get into his mouth in the first place. True, he had heard of dashing young gallants in the Gay Nineties quaffing champagne from the slippers of chorus girls, but he had never fancied the idea, did not care for champagne, doubted that a canvas shoe would hold whisky without ex-travagant leakage, and could recall nothing in the ritual that required a man to eat the footwear when he had drunk the whisky anyway. This hypothesis disposed of, he bethought him of a Hindu fakir he had once seen in Calcutta, as well as of various babies he had been unable to avoid in buses, railway carriages and other public places, all of whom could put their feet into their mouths as easily as Captain

Ball installed his false teeth. This led him to wonder if, in the course of the previous evening, he had
not won a bet by putting his foot into his mouth and
then inadvertently bitten it off. He lay pondering
the matter and finally he raised a groping hand to
investigate. He located his mouth with comparative
ease, and after a certain amount of fingering, probing
and kneading was able to establish beyond any reasonable doubt that the object within it was his tongue.

"Ah, dearie me!" he croaked. "I really must
try to cut doon on my smoking!"

Another source of acute discomfort was the
peculiar sense of constriction which beset his limbs
and body. His skin seemed to bind him, as though
it had shrunk; indeed, it felt so tight that he feared
it might split asunder, like the cover of a grilled
sausage. His head ached, too, and he realized that
while it was all very well to ignore the war in
principle, the bombardment still in progress made
the practical accomplishment difficult. As he lay
listening to it, the booming, crashing, banging and
blasting mounted to new and unexampled heights of
fury, until it seemed that all the bombs, torpedoes,
cannons, mortars, mines and other engines of de-
struction ever contrived by man were being touched
off right there beside him. Beside him? Nay, even
nearer than that! He pressed his hands to his throb-
bing temples and realized that the bombardment was
actually raging within the confines of his own cra-
nium.

"Ah, whurra, what frichtful misery!" he moaned. "Feerst my tongue is too big, then my skin is too small and noo my puir head is thrubbing lik' an owertaxed boiler!" He wondered whether he might not have contracted what he understood was vulgarly known as a hang-over, and had just dismissed the thought as preposterous and wholly unworthy of him, when he heard a key grate in a lock, a door open gently and the sound of shuffling feet. Succeeding after some effort in getting his eyelids unstuck, he found himself in darkness relieved only by a series of parallel streaks of pink light which he recognized as the dawn leaking in between the slats of a Venetian blind.

The footsteps approached across a tiled floor and halted at the bedside.

"Guid morning," said Mr. Glencannon tentatively, in a voice he was unable to recognize.

"Good evening," replied a voice which he recognized as Japanese.

"Eh? — What? — Evening?"

"Day-after-tomorrow evening," explained the Japanese voice. "Your Excellency sleep two night, sleep two day. Want I now pull up blinds?"

"Aye, go ahead, pull!" sighed Mr. Glencannon. "— I suppose I micht as weel learn the worst!"

As the blinds clicked up and the evening sunshine flooded in, he saw that he was lying in a spacious, handsomely furnished room, apparently one of a suite and that his visitor was an elderly messboy of the Nipponese Navy.

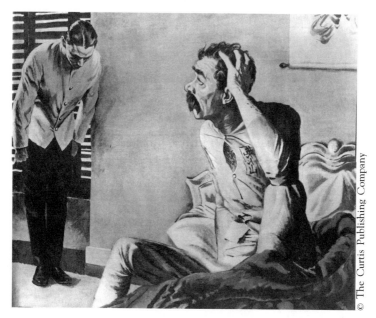

"Day after tomorrow evening," explained the Japanese voice. "Your excellency sleep two night, sleep two day. Want I now pull up blinds?"

"My name is Nogi," the Jap introduced himself, with a bow.

Slowly, with many a hollow groan, Mr. Glencannon rose from his bed of pain and made his way toward the window for air. Halfway there, however, the binding sensation which had for so long annoyed him turned into sheer, excruciating agony. Looking down at himself he saw that he was buttoned in a suit of scarlet silk pajamas which apparently had been tailored to fit a twelve-year-old boy. Even as he looked, a button popped and shot across the room.

"Shish-shish-shish!" simpered Nogi. "— Pajama of admiral Togawa very too tight for Your Excellency!"

"Never mind the cumpliments — they're too tight for me all ower!" growled Mr. Glencannon. "Quick, ye ape — dinna stond there snirtling aboot it! Help me get oot o' them before my varicose veins start exploding!"

Released from the thralldom of the pajamas, but with his body covered with welts, Mr. Glencannon completed his journey to the window without further incident. Bracing his feet and gripping the casement firmly, he ventured to look out. He was, he saw, on the sixth floor of the Royal Orient Hotel, Pandalang's leading caravansary. In the public gardens below, soldiers were digging shelter trenches in the flower beds and filling sandbags for revetments, while directly opposite, across the broad expanse of Lord Wellesley Square, was Government House. On the flagstaff that surmounted its cupola, the Rising Sun of Nippon stirred lazily in the breeze, looking for all the world like a squirming, blood-red octopus.

The nearer sections of the city appeared to have suffered only superficial damage, but all that remained of the Hao-kwan, Old Bazaar and East Pagoda quarters was a dismal, fire-blackened waste from which wraiths of smoke still rose like the mist from a tropic swamp. Shading his eyes, Mr. Glencannon peered out across these ruins in the direction of the Bund, half hoping that it was all a dream and that he would see the *Inchcliffe Castle* resting peacefully at her berth. In the place that she had occupied, three Japanese destroyers were tied up side by side, while out in the fairway beyond them eight more destroyers and a heavy cruiser lay at anchor. The latter was down by the stern and listing heavily. The S.S. *Inchcliffe Castle* was nowhere to be seen.

A great wave of loneliness, of bitter disillusionment, surged over Mr. Glencannon as he realized how treacherously the gods had betrayed him. Surely, he did not deserve — this! Swaying dizzily, he closed his eyes and gave vent to a choking sob.

"Shish-shish-shish!" came a sympathetic simper from behind him. "— Your Excellency still feel stinko? — Suppose I put raw egg in glass, put red pepper on egg, put Worcestershire sauce on red pepper, you drink *glup-glup*, make feel cheerio dam quick!"

"Eh? Why, that's a Mountain Oyster!" Mr. Glencannon turned and considered the servant with mingled curiosity and respect. "Weel, noo, my guid mon, what ye suggest is by no means devoid o' wisdom — but where in the world did ye learn that famous auld formula?"

"Oh, shish-shish, I bar steward ten year aboard ship *Nippon Yusen Kaisha* Line, make Mountain Oyster every morning, save lives ten thousand Englishmen."

Mr. Glencannon nodded pensively. "A-weel, I dinna doot that the prescription ye suggest is a hoonderd per cent effective on Englishmen, who are a nosty, drunken lot where'er ye find them. But o' course we Scots, being more delicately constituted, can only be revived with our own native medicament. Ah, losh!" His voice broke, his eyes filled and his hand trembled as with it he measured an imaginary drink. "What cuddn't I do to a dollop o' Dew the noo!"

"Dew?" repeated Nogi. "Your Excellency mean maybe Duggan Dew, same like are in closet?" He opened the door, disclosing the three familiar, fateful cases piled upon the floor.

"Aye! Aye! Aye, the vurra same!" cried Mr. Glencannon, starting forward wildly. "Quick, mon, open it up and pour it oot, or I willna onswer for the consequences!"

Perhaps ten minutes later, glass in hand and himself in the bathtub, he was making slow but sure progress along the road to recovery. The more he regained of his faculties, however, the more keenly he was able to appreciate the gravity of the situation. There were still a number of gaps in his memory; little by little, they were filling in, but, perversely, each newly remembered detail was just one more to worry about. What worried him most, of course, was the question of his own supposed identity.

"Who do they think I am?" he muttered. "— Or, to pose the prublem in another way, whom do they think I am?"

The bathroom door opened and in came Nogi. "I just finish telephone Commander Kaminashi, say you now all okay. Commander Kaminashi say very happy for you, come up see you soon."

"A-weel, that's vurra kind and sweet o' Commander Kaminashi," said Mr. Glencannon. "— Er! By the way, Nogi . . ." he peered at the Jap searchingly, "I hope ye pronounced my own name in a decent and civilized monner?"

"— Why, I say your name 'Admiral Sir Richard Keith-Frazer.' Is okay?"

"*Admiral?* Eh? What's that?" Mr. Glencannon hastily concealed his astonishment and most of his nose within his glass. "Aye!" he chuckled, finally coming up for air. "'Admiral Sir Richard Keith-Frazer' suits me vurra nicely, thonk ye!"

He emerged from the tub as fresh as Aphrodite rising from the waves, although considerably hairier. When he had shaved and dressed himself in the crisply starched uniform which Nogi laid out for him, he stood before the full-length mirror on the bathroom door and viewed his reflection with admiration and respect. "Losh, lad, ye're an admiral to yere vurra finger tips," he muttered. He looked down at the ribbons on his breast — five full rows of them — and meditated with modest pride on the deeds of courage and years of distinguished service that had put them there. He took up the cap, its visor embellished with golden oak leaves, and set it on his head at the rakish tilt affected by the officers of the Royal Navy. "Ho, dom, Glencannon!" he told himself, "Ye'd be fully capable o' taking the fleet to sea and winning the war this minute, if only ye weren't ignoring it!" A search of his pockets revealed that his brass knuckles were missing, and he concluded that they had been seized by the enemy. "No doot they've already shipped them home to Tokyo as battle trophies," he mused. "I suppose they'll exhibit them to the public in some national shrine or perhaps even hang them on the wall in the Emperor's throne room."

His ruminations were interrupted by a knock at his door, which Nogi opened to admit a personage whom he bowingly announced as Commander Kaminashi. This officer, who towered at least four feet eleven inches above the doorsill, was wearing a sword, the gold aiguillettes of an admiral's aide and a set of heavy caliber buck teeth. He saluted Mr. Glencannon, removed his cap, pressed it against his stomach and bowed over it three times. "Siss-s-s-s-s!" he said. Involuntarily, Mr. Glencannon glanced behind him to see if a cat were in the room.

"Sir. Admiral Yonizo Togawa presents his compliments to Admiral Sir Richard Keith-Frazer and requests the honor of his company at dinner," singsonged the newcomer.

"Oh, does he?" said Mr. Glencannon, with the considerable hauteur befitting his rank. "Weel, I must confess I'm no' owerly fond o' raw fish, kitten's eyes and all the other swill which you heathens eat for food, but as lang as I've nowt better to do, I suppose I micht as weel sit in an watch the admiral mak' himsel' sick. Tell me, Commander — will it be a dry party?"

"Oh, by no means, sir! By Admiral Togawa's order, I have made arrangements for a complete wine service."

"Then I'll tak' another guid sowp o' whusky before we start," said Mr. Glencannon. "— I was afraid it wud turn oot lik' that."

As they stepped into the corridor, a marine sentry posted at the door presented arms. The elevator was operated by a sailor, and as the car flashed down the shaft Mr. Glencannon caught glimpses of little white-uniformed men on every floor.

"We have taken over this hotel as our naval headquarters," Commander Kaminashi explained, with obvious pride. "The best the army could find for themselves was that dingy old Government House across the square. Shish-shish-shish!"

"Shish-shish-shish, by all means!" said Mr. Glencannon absently. He was busy wondering just what the Japanese game could be, as far as it concerned him in the role he was playing. Just what was there about Admiral Keith-Frazer which caused his captors to treat him with such marked consideration? Knowing Orientals as he did, he knew that they wanted something, and wanted it badly. But what? And what would they do to him if, as was likely, they found him unable to deliver it? Worst of all, what would they do to him when they discovered his true identity? "Whurra!" he shuddered. "I'm lik' an ox being fattened for the slaughter!"

They got off at the second floor and crossed the corridor into the royal suite. Passing through an outer reception room, now transformed into a staff office, they entered a salon at the center of which a little fat yellow man was seated at an enormous teakwood desk. Commander Kaminashi clicked his heels and came to attention. "Admiral Togawa, I have the distinguished honor of presenting Admiral Sir Richard Keith-Frazer, of the British Royal Navy," he chanted.

Admiral Togawa rose, but instead of hissing, bowing and scraping in the formal Japanese manner, he smiled and waved a pudgy hand in what apparently was intended to be a bluff and breezy gesture of welcome from one old sea dog to another. "A pleasure, Admiral — a great pleasure, I'm sure!" he said, attempting, without notable success, to impart a basso quality to his naturally squeaky voice. "Make yourself comfortable in that chair, Admiral! I hope you're feeling fit, sir?"

"So do I, thonk ye!" said Mr. Glencannon, seating himself and taking rapid stock of his host. "Haw, Admiral — I'll tell ye what I'll do with ye! Just for the fun o' it, I'll bet ye three quid here and noo that I've got more medals than you've got! What d'ye say?"

"Ah, no doubt, no doubt!" Admiral Togawa smiled jovially, proceeding to fill an English brier pipe from a tin of English tobacco and lighting it with an English patent lighter. "After all, my dear Keith-Frazer, you chaps are several up on us when it comes to actual fighting experience. — At least, so far! . . ." He strolled around from behind the desk and stood with his tiny, white-shod feet spread wide apart, his hands thrust deep into his jacket pockets and his pipe cocked up at a jaunty angle. He reminded Mr. Glencannon of a ludicrous but unkind caricature of something, but for the moment he was unable to say exactly what.

"How about a little spot of whisky, old boy?" inquired the Jap, and Mr. Glencannon realized that his host had a comfortable load aboard already. "I always leave the matter of the wine list to my aide, but you may be sure I attend to the whisky myself, ha-ha!" From the desk he brought out a bottle and two glasses, and placed them on a tray beside the thermos pitcher. Mr. Glencannon saw that the bottle bore the Duggan label — saw it with mixed emotions, for keenly though he craved a snifter, the thought of this pudgy yellow caricature partaking of the honest Highland nectar seemed to him a sacrilege. And suddenly he recognized what the Jap had been caricaturing all along; *a Briton!* Mr. Glencannon's brow beetled. "Ah, foosh!" he fumed to himself. "The impudence, the insolence o' the vulgar little snirk. Why, no doot he's been studying and working and trying to perfect his imitation o' a Briton for years. He's been making himsel' sick on white mon's tobacco and whusky, spraining his jaw on white mon's talk, warping his dwarfed carcass trying to stond and walk and act lik' a British officer — when all the time the Guid Lord intended him to hong by his tail in a coconut tree! A-weel! . . ."

Admiral Togawa had poured the drinks, and now raised his own. "Well, cheerio, chin-chin, pip-pip and all that sort of rot!" he said in his best P.G. Wodehouse manner.

Mr. Glencannon also raised his glass, but said nothing. Instead, deliberately and impressively, as though observing a rite, he tilted back his head, drew a long breath and spat upon the ceiling. Then, and not until then, did he consume his drink.

Although it was an important part of Admiral Togawa's imitation of a Briton never to evince surprise, he could not conceal the fact that this performance startled him. "Er, I say! . . ."

"Braugh!" Mr. Glencannon interrupted him, setting down his empty glass. "I congrotulate ye on yere whusky, sir! It has lang been my contention that Duggan's Dew o' Kirkintilloch is a superior and most exceptional product — the unvarying choice o' discriminating connoisseurs in clubs, bars, private homes, and, in fact, wherever an aged, mellowed and truly select Scotch whusky is appreciated."

"— Eh? Oh, yes — quite, quite!" Admiral Togawa hastily recalled his attention from the ceiling. "Yes, Duggan's Dew — 'D.D.,' as we old whisky bibbers like to call it — is really not too bad, is it? What d'you say we blot up another before we bung in to dinner?"

"I say we blot," said Mr. Glencannon.

This time, Admiral Togawa kept one eye on Mr. Glencannon and the other on the ceiling, resolved that no part of the ceremony should escape him.

"By Jove, Keith-Frazer!" he exclaimed, no longer able to restrain his curiosity. "That's a jolly unusual stunt of yours! Quaint, I mean to say!"

"Stunt?" Mr. Glencannon looked at him blankly. "Quaint? Ah, o' course, o' course! Ye really must forgive me, Admiral, for absent-mindedly obsairving an auld Royal Naval custom o' whuch ye're necessarily ignorant."

"Oh, let's not say I'm — ignorant!" The Jap squirmed in his chair. "— I've made a deep study of all your ancient naval customs, but that one — well, that one seems to have slipped my mind for the moment."

"A-weel, it harks back to the time o' the auld, antique frigates," Mr. Glencannon explained graciously, "to the days o' *iron men and wouldn't ships*, as the poet Masefield so nobly expresses it, though be domned if it mak's much sense to me. However, in order to prevent the red-hot cannon balls o' that primitive period from setting fire to the deck owerhead, it was customarra for all hands below to spit on the ceiling as frequently and copiously as possible. Today, o' course, it's purely a gesture, symbolical o' devotion to the ship."

"Ah, yes, yes, of course! A charming old tradition! I knew I'd heard of it somewhere!" beamed the admiral, hastening to fill the glasses. He handed one to Mr. Glencannon and then, bracing himself, attempted to emulate him in performing the ritual. He failed ignominiously.

"Haw, losh, ye missed it a mile!" Mr. Glencannon chided him. "Ye have to put more steam behind it mon! Ye must learn to force yere gizzard doon upon yere diaphragm and snop yere shoulders forward the instant ye let go."

Admiral Togawa was stung to the quick by this taunt. "Now wait, wait!" he cried, petulantly. "I'm a bit out of practice, that's all. Come we'll try again!" It was not until his fourth try, however, that he succeeded. "There!" he gloated, patting himself on the chest. "I knew I could do it! Now we can go in to dinner!"

According to Japanese standards, Admiral Togawa had saved his face.

The monkey had learned a new trick.

4

As was to be expected of the Anglophile Admiral Togawa, the dinner he provided turned out to be a somewhat exaggerated imitation of an English meal. Mr. Glencannon barged into it with gusto, in spite and because of a lurking premonition that it might well be his last.

"I do hope everything's to your liking, old chap," the Jap was saying solicitously. "After the knocking about that those fools in our army bombers gave your place the other night, the least I can do is give you a decent dinner."

"Aye?" said Mr. Glencannon, noncommittally, helping himself to another slab of Yorkshire pudding.

"Oh, absolutely! They had explicit orders to drop nothing but fragmentations on the dockyard, but the silly blighters went right ahead and loosed off some fairly heavy H.E. on you."

"Aye?"

"Why, yes, didn't you notice? Oh, and by the way, Keith-Frazer, that brings us to a little point I was intending to mention. Of course you won't mind collaborating with us for a bit, until we can get the yards back into operation, will you?"

Mr. Glencannon looked at him questioningly.

"Yes, just for a week or so," the Jap continued. "You see, not only is there a certain amount of damage that must be repaired, thanks to those damned army chumps of ours, but there is a lot of machinery and mechanical equipment among the installations that we simply don't know anything about. And so I thought. . . ."

"But. . . ."

"But naturally! After all, my dear fellow, you are the genius who made the Victoria Point naval base what it is! You know more about the establishment than any other man alive! If you'll just give us the benefit of your knowledge until we get the hang of things — well, we'd be grateful no end!"

"— And if I shud be forced to decline?"

Admiral Togawa spread his pudgy hands and smiled pleasantly. "Oh, in that case you will be shot," he said.

Mr. Glencannon gulped, turned pale and endeavored to finish chewing a mouthful of roast

Admiral Togawa spread his pudgy hands and smiled pleasantly. "Oh, in that case you will be shot," he said.

beef with his palate. "Ho, dom!" he protested, choking. "What a — a b-barbarous suggestion!"

"The fortunes of war, old fellow! But come, be reasonable! Say you'll help us!"

Mr. Glencannon mopped the sweat from his forehead and the gravy from his chin. "Just exoctly what wud ye expect me to do?" he asked weakly.

"Well, your first job — rather urgent — would be to superintend repairs on Number Three Dry Dock. Some fool scored a direct hit on the gate, and now we can't budge it. It's a fearfully complicated mechanism, as you know."

Mr. Glencannon shook his head. "No, I dinna know a single thing aboot it."

"What? Oh, tut, tut, my dear fellow; I suppose you'll even try to tell me you've never heard of the Keith-Frazer Rolling Caisson Gate! But please don't, because we happen to know that you, personally, designed that dock, the gate, the pumps and all the rest of it!"

Mr. Glencannon leaned across the table and looked him straight in the eye. "Admiral Togawa," he said impressively, "through no fault o' mine, there's been a frichtful mistake. Please dinna osk me to explain it, because I can't. I can only assure ye from my ain feersthond knowledge that I am not Admiral Sir Richard Keith-Frazer and, what's more, I've never claimed to be. Surely — surely, ye canna shoot me for that!"

For a moment, Admiral Togawa seemed on the verge of losing his patience. "You've been drinking!" he said.

"Noturally, I've been drinking — there's whusky aroond! But if ye still think I'm Admiral Keith-Frazer, I chollenge ye to send for some o' his officers richt this minute and osk them if they ever set eyes on me before!"

Admiral Togawa shrugged. "Most of them escaped, worse luck! Anyway, what you suggest wouldn't prove a thing. If you were childish enough to cook up this denial of your identity in the event of your capture, I've no doubt you ordered your officers to back you up in it. Er, but wait — yes, come to think of it, we've got another prisoner, an outsider whose testimony will, I hope, convince you of your error in playing me for a fool." He took up the telephone from the side table and chattered an order in Japanese.

With a heartfelt sigh of relief, Mr. Glencannon sat back in his chair. "Ah, swith! — Thonk heaven, I've saved my life, at any rate!" he congratulated himself. "No matter who this other prisoner turns oot to be, he surely willna mistake me for the Admiral!"

The other prisoner turned out to be a khaki-clad American commander with a stitched-up gash on his forehead and a scowl on his face. He was flanked by two shoulder-high Marines with fixed bayonets.

"Ah!" said Admiral Togawa. "You are Commander Thomas Barry, U.S.N.? — A dry-dock-construction engineer of the United States Navy

Bureau of Yards and Docks on liaison duty with the British?"

"What is it to you?" snapped the American.

"Please control your temper, Commander — I know perfectly well who you are. I merely want to ask if you recognize this officer here."

Commander Barry turned toward Mr. Glencannon and started violently. "Oh! Why — yes, sure I recognize him!" he said. "He's Admiral Sir Richard Keith-Frazer, R.N."

Admiral Togawa beamed and rubbed his hands. "Ah, precisely! No chance of your being mistaken, commander?"

"Of course not! Are you all okay, Admiral Keith-Frazer? How are they treating you? — You're — you're looking a little faint, sir!"

As a matter of fact, Mr. Glencannon had fainted. When he regained his senses he found himself being supported from the room by Commander Kaminashi and a pair of sailors.

" . . . And furthermore," Admiral Togawa was screaming after him, his voice cold and shrill, "furthermore, I'm sick of you and your nonsense! You can think it over tonight and send me your decision in the morning. — Think it over carefully, sir — yes, very, very carefully! And don't forget the alternative, my dear Admiral Sir Richard Keith-Frazer!"

Mr. Glencannon's escort took him up in the elevator to the door of his suite, checked him past the sentry and turned him over to Nogi. "Shish-

shish-shish!" simpered the messboy, assisting him to
an armchair. "Your Excellency get all stunk up
again, isn't?"

"No, isn't in the least," Mr. Glencannon assured him dismally. "Still, it's a guid idea, so fetch
the bottle and leave me alone with my sorrow."

He sat for a long time, drinking, thinking and
drinking. The longer he thought, the more terrible
his predicament appeared. "Alas, Colin lad, ye're in
for it this time!" he told himself. "With all yer
genius, ye canna ignore a war when it comes leaping
at ye oot o' the muzzles o' a dozen rifles and ye've
got yere back against a brick wall. If only. . . ."

He heard the tramp of martial feet approaching in the hall. They halted outside the door. "Ah,
whurra!" he moaned, cringing behind the bottle. "Are
they going to shoot me noo instead o' waiting till
the customarra sunrise?"

The door opened and in came Commander
Kaminashi, followed by Commander Barry.

"Admiral Keith-Frazer," said the Jap, "Admiral Togawa has assigned Commander Thomas Barry
to you as your personal aide. He directs me to
convey his earnest hope that American common
sense will overcome British bullheadedness — shish-
shish! I bid you good night, gentlemen!" The door
closed after him.

"Well, Admiral, how are you feeling now,
sir?" Barry demanded loosely. "It was too bad you
got so upset awhile ago, because that Jap admiral is
really a pretty decent little guy. He. . . ."

With a hoarse cry, Mr. Glencannon sprang to his feet and stood trembling with rage. He would have clouted Barry with the bottle had he not prudently realized that the fellow was big enough and tough enough to reduce him to cat's meat, even though wounded in the forehead. "Ah, foosh to ye!" he snarled. "Luckily for you, my sense o' sportsmonship prevents me from striking a cripple! Otherwise, I'd — I'd . . . ! — Weel . . . !" He shifted his grip on the bottle and proceeded to put it to orthodox use.

"Yes, yes! Of course, Admiral!" Commander Barry spoke as though addressing an audience. "— Of course you're sore at me for spilling the beans and identifying you. But Admiral Togawa knew perfectly well who you were, and. . . ."

"Blosh and fuddlesticks!" roared Mr. Glencannon, uncoupling his mouth from the bottle. "He. . . ."

Commander Barry's hand shot forward and muffled the mouth like a gag. "Pipe down, you fool," he whispered fiercely. "Wait till I see if they've rigged a dictaphone on us!" He tiptoed around the room, looking behind pictures and furniture. Very gently he dragged the dresser a few inches out from the wall, then grinned and beckoned. Mr. Glencannon joined him and peered behind the mirror. Attached to the back of it by means of a rubber suction cup, he saw a black metal object the size of a watch. A wire no thicker than a heavy thread extended down from it, disappearing into the crack between the floor tiles and the wall.

"Yes, Admiral," Barry resumed in his loud voice, at the same time nodding and winking, "after they brought you back up here, Admiral Togawa and I had a long talk, man to man, and — well, he showed me what fools we'd be not to play ball with him. It's that gate on Number Three Dry Dock that worries him most. Of course, they can probably fix it in a day or so, without us — so what's the sense of getting ourselves shot just for honor and glory and all that old-fashioned hooey?" He cupped his hand close to Mr. Glencannon's ear. "Come on, now," he whispered. "Speak up and pretend you're being persuaded."

"Er, weel," said Mr. Glencannon, dazed but obedient, "O' course I dinna wholly approve o' yere attitude, my boy, but I must confess there's a guid deal o' sense in what ye say. After all, as ye point oot, the Jops can fix the gate by themselves with vurra little extra trouble, and our getting shot certainly canna prevent them."

"Then you mean you'll help, sir?"

"Why not?"

"Fine! That's settled! I'll sleep a lot better tonight knowing I don't have to face a firing squad in the morning! Yo-ho-hum!" he yawned. "Speaking of sleep, what do you say we hit the hay, sir?"

The beds were at the far side of the room, well removed from the dictaphone, but the two prisoners continued to whisper as they lay in the darkness.

"Young mon," said Mr. Glencannon severely, "I dinna ken exoctly how I hoppened to get into this mess in the feerst place, but I do know that ye've shoved me into it deeper. If it were no' for the state o' fatigue I'm in, I'd come ower there and tromple oot yere liver."

"Oh, you would?" Barry chuckled. "Well, tell me, Mr. MacWalrus, or whatever your name is — how would you like to connect with another good sock on the jaw?"

"Another?" Mr. Glencannon bristled. "— What do ye mean, 'another'?"

Commander Barry did not answer. Instead, very softly, he sang the opening bar of an old Scottish ballad: *My love is lik' a red, red rose . . .* "Well?" he inquired after a pause. "Does that remind you of — anything?"

"A-weel, I know the song, o' course. As a matter o' fact, I was singing it rather tunefully, just the other evening, when — when . . ." Suddenly, the events of the night of the bombardment began coming back to Mr. Glencannon in a trickle of recollection. He remembered a car in a narrow, rubble-blocked street. He remembered an admiral standing beside it. He remembered a khaki-clad officer who had stepped from the shadows into his path and landed a haymaker on his chin without so much as a by-your-leave. "Foosh, ye thug, so it was you," he whispered, tremulously. "— Feerst ye knock me unconscious, then ye disguise me as an admiral, then ye get me captured! Next ye come butting in when I've all but cleared mysel' with the Jop and try to get me shot! Heaven only knows what calomity ye're planning for me noo, but I'd lik' an explanation!"

Commander Barry gave him an account of all that had happened on the night of Pandalang's fall. "And now," he concluded, "I'm going to make a hero of you whether you like it or not — a greater hero than you are already! Why, just think of what you've done, man! Thanks to you, Admiral Keith-Frazer escaped capture, got out to the fleet and shot hell out of a Jap task force! I heard them talking about it among themselves downstairs and. . . ."

"— What? Ye mean ye understond Joponese?"

"Yes, sure; my dad was consul in Nagasaki for eleven years. Well, anyway, one of the ships Keith-Frazer shot up was their new heavy cruiser *Tsushima*. She's lying out here in the harbor now with a twenty-degree list on her, and I heard 'em saying if they can't get her into that Number Three Dry Dock pronto, she's likely to sink at her moorings."

"What's wrong with the other dry docks?"

"They're all too small for her."

"Why don't they beach her, then?"

"Because everything around here is coral bottom and they'd simply rip her keel off. She's so far down by the stern that there isn't deep enough water to get her alongside any of the wharfs. So now you see why you and I are going to fix that Number

Three Dry Dock gate — fix it good, fix it for keeps — fix it so these yellowbellies will be shy exactly one new heavy cruiser!"

"H'm," in the darkness, Mr. Glencannon gnawed at the fringes of his mustache. "Just what do ye think we can do to it?"

"Well, the British had the dry dock all mined and ready to blow up. For some reason, they didn't touch it off. Apparently, the Japs haven't yet discovered the demolition charges in Number Three's gate — though why the stuff didn't explode when their bomb hit, I don't know. But tomorrow, you and I are going down inside that gate and find out!"

"Ah, swith," said Mr. Glencannon, stricken with awe. "Ye mean we'll blow it up and oursel's alang with it?"

"Why not? We'd be a pretty fair exchange for a new heavy cruiser, wouldn't we?"

There was a long pause.

"A-weel," said Mr. Glencannon, "that all depends on how highly ye value yersel'. Pairsonally, I consider a mon o' my caliber to be worth at least a battleship and two aircraft carriers, and I have no slichtest intention o' blowing mysel' to smithereens for a mere cruiser."

"Oh, no? Hey, listen, bud," said Barry grimly. "If either of us is still alive after that gate blows up ·— well, he won't stay alive very long, or I don't know Japs."

"So?" Mr. Glencannon's tone was polite but skeptical. "Just exoctly how weel do ye think ye know them?"

"I lived among them from the time I was seven until the year before I went to the Naval Academy. Still, I don't suppose any white man can ever really understand the monkeys. They're imitative, sure, but at the same time they're — unpredictable. Why, tonight, for instance, after little Big-Shot Togawa and I had finished our powwow, he suggested that we seal the bargain with a drink. He hoisted his glass as though he was going to offer a toast — and what do you suppose he did then?"

"He spit on the ceiling, o' course."

"— Hunh?" Commander Barry sat upright in the darkness. "See here," he whispered. "How in blazes do you know that?"

"Sumply because I know the Joponese," said Mr. Glencannon loftily.

There was a long moment of silence, broken only by the sound of Commander Barry scratching his head. "Well, say," he demanded at length. "Just exactly who do you happen to be, anyway?"

"A-weel," came a chuckle from the other bed, "I micht hoppen to be the Richt Honorable Winston Churchill or I micht hoppen to be the Archbishop o' Canterbury. As a matter o' fact, however, I am Muster Colin Glencannon, Esquire, and I intend to continue as such until the end o' the chopter."

5

Shortly after dawn they were aroused by Nogi. "Shish-shish-shish, good morning!" he greeted them. "Commander Kaminashi say very sorry make wake so early. He come see you very soon." He set down a tray of breakfast things, then opened the blinds, turned on the bath and pattered out.

Mr. Glencannon seated himself at the table and poured himself some fragrant Japanese tea, which he was careful to dilute with an adequate quantity of whisky. Yawning and stretching, Commander Barry strolled over to the window.

"Well, it looks like a pleasant morning, Admiral!" he called, at the same time pointing toward the dresser to remind Mr. Glencannon of the dictaphone. "— Er!" he beckoned excitedly.

"Look!" he whispered, when the other had joined him. "Look at that cruiser now! Why, she's listed another five degrees overnight. See how they've got her turrets swung around to put the weight of the guns on the high side? They've got all her starboard boats in the water too. Boy, oh, boy — if they can't trim her up a little pretty soon, she'll turn turtle sure as hell!"

"Aye — and vurra noturally they're frontic," nodded Mr. Glencannon, returning to his tea. "It explains why they routed up us two chompion dry-dock fixers in the midst o' our beauty sleep."

They had scarcely finished dressing when Commander Kaminashi came bustling in. "Good morning, Admiral! Good morning, commander!" he said briskly. "Admiral Togawa sends his most distinguished compliments to Admiral Keith-Frazer and trusts that he has reached a favorable decision in the matter of. . . ."

"Aye!" Mr. Glencannon interrupted. "Ye can deliver my even more distinguished compliments to Admiral Togawa and tell him I'm all set to fix his dry dock for him at the drop o' a lamb's tail."

"Ah, I am so very happy to hear it!" said Kaminashi, although it was obvious that he had heard it long before. He walked over to the window, looked out and then nervously consulted his wrist watch. "Well, if you gentlemen are ready," he said, edging toward the door, "the car is waiting down-stairs."

In the course of the nine-mile ride across the city and suburbs to Victoria Point, they met dozens of tanks, hundreds of trucks and endless columns of infantry, all moving southward, as well as swarms of native refugees straggling back to what was left of their homes. Once they passed a long line of British prisoners, mostly civilians, plodding along through the dust. A few of them, spotting an admiral's uniform, shook their fists after the car and shouted unkind words about the bloody, blundering brasshat.

"Ho, dom!" growled Mr. Glencannon, who was feeling his breakfast, "Have the unsubordinate louts got no respect for my rank and dignity? — If I had them under my command for ten minutes, doon in the *Inchcliffe Castle's* stokehold, I'd teach them who was who!"

Commander Barry jabbed an elbow into his ribs. "Pipe down!" he whispered, savagely.

They crossed the drawbridge over Kulong Creek and entered the dockyard. From each of the old crenelated stone gate towers, the Japanese flag was flying. As they passed along roadways flanked by great, grimy sheds of brick and corrugated iron, with towering chimneys and jutting cranes, Mr. Glencannon was reminded of the Clydeside shops where, in his youth, he had served his time as apprentice. He felt that the only false notes were the clear blue sky and blazing tropical sunshine which replaced the good old clammy Glasgow murk. "Ah, swith!" he sighed nostalgically. "What wuddn't I give this minute for a whiff o' the fog and the tidal mud!"

Although here and there gangs of native civilian prisoners were filling up bomb craters, clearing away rubble and spreading tarpaulins over gaping holes in roofs and walls, the place appeared to be but little damaged. The car turned into a road which paralleled the shore of Victoria Cove and stopped at the control tower on the rim of Number Three Dry Dock.

In the course of his travels around and about the world, it had been Mr. Glencannon's privilege to behold many of man's truly superlative works. He had stood in the arena of the Colosseum and meditated on the grandeur that was Rome, until convinced by a policeman that he was actually in the Acropolis at Athens. From the brink of the Big Hole Diamond Mine at Kimberly, he had peered into the abyss with one eye while keeping the other peeled for any stray solitaires that might be within filching distance. He had seen the Sphinx and the Pyramids, though not very distinctly, and had expectorated times without number into the Panama and Suez canals. All these and other wonders he had seen, but never, never had he gazed upon a dry dock comparable to Pandalang's vast number three. It was twelve hundred feet long and one hundred and fifty feet wide. Its floor lay sixty feet below the level at which he stood. Down on that floor, an area of more than four acres, at least five hundred Japanese sailors were swarming and toiling like ants as they secured huge balks and steel frames which electric cranes were lowering into place.

"Look at 'em," whispered Barry. "— Just look at 'em! They're sweating blood to get the keel blocks and bilge supports all set, so they won't lose a second getting that cruiser in!" He turned to Commander Kaminashi. "Well, come on, you!" he said brusquely. "Admiral Keith-Frazer is ready to examine the gate."

The gate was a mammoth steel caisson, mounted on rails, which, in its present closed position, prevented the waters of Victoria Cove from flooding into the dock basin. It was operated by hydraulic rams which normally were capable of shifting its thousand-odd tons of weight as easily as a man slides open a well-oiled garage door. But now, like the average garage door, the gate refused to budge. A group of grimy, overalled engineer officers and machinist petty officers were standing on the platform near the control tower, looking down at it in baffled disgust, and bickering among themselves. Apparently they had been working all night. At sight of the new arrivals, they ceased their chatter and came forward eagerly. Commander Kaminashi addressed them in Japanese, whereupon they all faced Mr. Glencannon and bowed as one man.

"Weel, weel, weel, a vurra guid morning to ye!" he returned the greeting, rubbing his hands and turning on his most magnificent smile. "Noo, gentlemen, just what seems to be the difficulty this beautiful, sunny morning? A little gate trouble, is that it? Ah, I see, I see! H'm. Tsk-tsk-tsk! Weel, noo, ye really mustn't let yersel's worrit aboot a sumple trifle lik' that! Just sit doon and relox yersel's gentlemen, or go ower there in the shade and curl up with a guid book. My friend and I will fix things up in no time, if ye'll only get to hell oot o' our way and stop bothering us!"

Barry followed him down the narrow steps in the concrete which led to the top of the gate. The steel surface was nearly as wide as the deck of a destroyer; on one side, almost level with it, the ripples of Victoria Cove slapped gently against the plates, while on the other was a sheer drop of sixty feet to the dock floor. At intervals there were hatchways down which vertical iron ladders led to the buoyancy chambers and mechanism housings deep within the structure. Almost at the center — a beautiful shot! — was a yawning, jagged-edged hole where the bomb had struck.

"Losh, a fair bull's-eye!" said Mr. Glencannon, approaching as near as he dared to the edge of it and looking down. "The Jop who scored that hit must have won the special presentation trophy o' cold boiled rice with fish heads!"

"Oh, yes? I'll make you a little bet that if they didn't shoot him, it's only because he beat them to it! Come on — let's go below."

They clambered down one of the hatchway ladders to the first level. With its ripped and twisted plates and clutters of debris, it looked rather like the

© The Curtis Publishing Company

"Noo, gentlemen, just what seems to be the difficulty this beautiful, sunny morning? A little gate trouble, is that it?"

interior of a torpedoed ship. "It won't be here," muttered Barry, taking a quick look about him. "We've got to go lower."

Mr. Glencannon followed him to the next level, which was brilliantly lighted by electricity and comparatively little damaged. "Weel," he said, "except for these giant valves and pumps, all I can see here is a certain amoont o' water trickling in through the seams betwixt the plates, and all I can smell is roncid grease, anti-corrosive paint and the frowsty odor o' owerworked Jops. Exoctly what are we looking for, lad?"

Commander Barry pointed at an oblong object lying in the angle of the deck and bulkhead. "For that!" he said exultantly. Stooping to examine it, Mr. Glencannon saw a metal case about the size of a wardrobe trunk. It was painted dark gray, and on the top of it was stenciled:

Plan K
No. 3 Gate

"What's inside it?" he asked.

"Five hundred pounds of TNT. I s'pose the Japs thought it was a tool chest. But — but look, damn the luck! The detonator is all set, but it isn't wired up! Oh, jumping jeepus, what a lousy break! How in the world are we ever going to explode it?"

"That," said Mr. Glencannon, "is entirely oot o' my department."

"Oh, Lord!" groaned Barry, crouching down and peering into the tubular brass fitting, something like a sawed-off hose nozzle, which projected from the end of the chest. "The detonator's so far inside the socket I can't even reach it with my finger. We've got to think of something! H'm — let's see now. . . . Supposing I just shove a lighted match. . . . . It's a thousand to one it won't work, but — but give me a match, Glencannon!"

"Tush, lad, it's dangerous to play with motches. Why tak' foolish risks, when a pairfect solution is shining right square in yere eyes?"

"Hunh? What do you mean?"

Mr. Glencannon waved his hand toward the electric light on the bulkhead beside them. "There's what I mean," he said. "Noo, listen, Thomas — listen carefully and get this! Feerst, I'll go up above to the control tower, saying I've got to check the electric-power leads. I'll turn off the juice at the main switch. As soon as the lights go oot, you rip that conduit loose and poke the wires into the detonator socket, d'ye see? Then ye must come richt up and tell Kaminashi ye've located the trouble — and also that ye've found an unexploded bomb buried in the wreckage caused by the other one. O' course ye'll be vurra angry aboot this, and demond to know what the hell they meant by letting us go doon there before they'd made a thorough search. Ye must insist that they remove the dud bomb, so ye can go on with yere work. At the opportune moment, I'll close the switch and. . . ."

"— *Pow!* Oh, boy! That's great! That's marvelous! That's — that's *it!*" Commander Barry gripped him by the hand. "Well, hop to it, pardner!"

As Mr. Glencannon emerged from the hatchway, Commander Kaminashi came hurrying anxiously across the gate top to meet him. "Well, Admiral?" he asked, "Have you found the trouble?"

"I think so," said Mr. Glencannon, frowning and pursing his lips. "However, I'll have to climb up into yon control tower and look things ower a bit before I can let ye know definitely."

He located the switch without difficulty, pulled it open, and then went puttering about the little steel cabin, pretending to be busy. A car stopped at the base of the tower and from it stepped Admiral Togawa and an army officer. He watched as they descended to the top of the gate and walked out to the bomb hole near the center. From their gestures, Mr. Glencannon could tell that an acrimonious discussion was in progress.

After what seemed an hour, but was perhaps ten minutes, he saw Barry climb out of the hatch and nod. The admiral beckoned to him and the three stood talking. Then, suddenly, Togawa stiffened, turned and headed for the dock rim, dragging Barry by the arm. They were closely followed by the army officer.

"Haw!" chuckled Mr. Glencannon. "Tommy has told them aboot the dud, and they dinna foncy the idea o' having it so close beneath the seats o' their breeks!"

At the foot of the tower, Togawa summoned the overalled technicians to gather around him and launched into a spirited harangue. Evidently he was reprimanding them for overlooking the unexploded bomb and translating Barry's directions for finding it under the wreckage. At the conclusion, he waved them imperiously toward the gate.

Mr. Glencannon waited until the last of the Japs had disappeared into the hatchway. He took a final look at the blue sky, at the deep, breeze-rippled water outside the gate and at the swarm of laborers toiling on the dock floor within it. "A-weel," he drew a long breath, "noo is as guid a time as any!" He crouched, braced himself and closed the switch.

His eardrums shivered and his stomach winced. The tower whipped over to a crazy angle and stayed there. Gasping as though he had been kicked in the diaphragm, Mr. Glencannon clawed his way back to the window. Through a cloud of yellow smoke, he saw a mighty, raging torrent burst into the dock, go charging down the length of it and crash against the far wall, where it leaped a hundred feet into the air. Then came a backwash almost as terrible as the first great wave itself, and for minutes on end the filthy brown water continued to surge to and fro. But gradually the turmoil subsided to a gentle heaving, and the surface became dotted with floating objects. There were timbers, balks, keel blocks — and hundreds of other things. . . .

A siren was wailing. From all over the yards, men came rushing to the dockside. Mr. Glencannon climbed down the twisted struts of the tower just as Barry and the Japs were getting to their feet. They were still half stunned.

"How are ye, Tommy, lad?" asked Mr. Glencannon, offering his arm for support. "Are ye hurt?"

"I'm — I'm okay, I guess. — Yes, I'm all okay! And — boy, oh, *boy!*"

Suddenly, Admiral Togawa, pale to the lips with rage, commenced screaming at the army officer and shaking his fist in his face. His British veneer had cracked and fallen from him. The tirade went on and on. When at length he regained control of himself, he turned to Mr. Glencannon and Barry. "Gentlemen," he said slowly, "you have just seen the stupidity of another branch of the service bring black disgrace to the Imperial Nipponese Navy." He bowed. "Commander Kaminashi will conduct you back to the hotel."

Mr. Glencannon and Commander Barry sat in their room near the open window, their feet and a bottle on the table and joy in their hearts. They had just ripped the dictaphone from the back of the dresser mirror and tossed it down into Lord Wellesley Square.

". . . That little army guy was an Air Corps colonel," Barry was explaining. "When I came up out of the hatchway on top of the gate, Togawa was giving him hell about his pilots dropping bombs where they'd been ordered not to, and the Colonel was swearing by the sacred tails of his monkey ancestors that the whole thing was an accident. He had an alibi all cooked up about defective bomb racks, and when Togawa translated what I said about a dud bomb still being down there, he did some quick thinking and said sure, sure, that just proved his case! According to him, the two bombs must've come loose by themselves, but the cocking trip on the busted mechanism had only armed one of them. Togawa didn't fall for it a nickel's worth. He called the colonel nine kinds of liar and promised to report him to Tokyo. — After the gate blew up, of course, he put him under arrest."

"Haw!" chuckled Mr. Glencannon. "A-weel, Tommy, we did a vurra neat morning's work, after all. Come, noo, confess it, lad — dinna ye feel a wee bit healthier than ye wud have felt if ye'd blown yersel' to bits alang with the gate?"

"I'll say!" Barry raised his arms and expanded his biceps. "And besides — " he leaned over to the window and peered out, " — and besides, er . . . Oh! Hey, look at 'er now! Quick, feller!"

Mr. Glencannon looked and saw that the wounded cruiser *Tsushima* had not long to live. Two destroyers were standing by helplessly and the water all around her was dotted with boats and life rafts. Suddenly dozens, then scores, of little white splashes commenced flicking up the water close to her side. "Swith — they're jumping owerboard," he muttered. "Look, Tommy, she's heeling ower more and more

He leaned over to the window and peered out — "and besides — er — Oh! Hey, look at 'er now! Quick, feller!"

— faster and faster! Hoot, mon! There — there — *there she goes!"*

With a snoring sob that could be heard half across Pandalang, the great ship thrashed over on her back, water cascading from her bilge keels. For perhaps half a minute she lay with her belly in the air, rolling obscenely; then, stern first, she slid out of sight. Where she had been, there was only a seething patch of white.

Without a word, Mr. Glencannon and Commander Barry faced each other and gripped hands. It was a long, muscular handshake and, when they broke it off, they reached for the bottle in unison.

"No, pairmit me!" said Mr. Glencannon, getting a stranglehold on the neck of it. "I'm really
vurra guid at pouring!"

It was not until after three o'clock that Nogi
came in with the lunch. As he wheeled the little
chromium-plated serving cart up to the table, his
shish-shish-shish was missing and he appeared to be
upset.

"What's the matter, Nogi? Heard from yere
wife?" inquired Mr. Glencannon, evincing polite
interest.

"Very bad day!" said Nogi, shaking his head
dolefully. "Dry dock blow up, kill five hundred and
thirty man. *Tsushima* sink, sixty-three man drown.
Admiral Togawa and Colonel Shimoku both two
commit *hara-kiri*, both two dead. Very bad day!"

"Oh, come, come — ye mustna be so pessi-
mistic!" Mr. Glencannon admonished him. "If only
more people wud mak' up their minds to ignore the
war, lik' I do, just think what a lovely world this
wud be."

When they had finished eating, and Nogi,
still depressed, had taken his departure, Mr.
Glencannon resumed where he had left off with the
bottle. "A-weel, Thomas," he said thoughtfully, "there
dinna seem to be any more dry docks, cruisers, ad-
mirals or colonels to occupy our talents — ye'll
notice, o' course that I scorn to mention the smaller
fry — so I'm wondering just what our next move is
to be."

"— Into a barb wire stockade, where we'll live on rice and rats till the end of the war," said Barry. "— That is, if we're lucky. But with Togawa gone soaring aloft to the heavenly monkey house to meet his curator, there's no telling exactly what the new administration will do with us."

"What they'll do *to* us, ye mean!" said Mr. Glencannon ominously. "— Especially to me, when they finally find oot I'm no' an admiral."

"Yes, and to me — when they remember I positively identified you as one." Commander Barry sighted along the barrel of an imaginary rifle. "*Br-r-rang!*" he imitated the ragged volley of a firing squad.

"Ah, whurra! Shut up!" Mr. Glencannon shuddered. "— Canna ye think o' something more pleasant for us to worrit aboot?"

"Well, yes, as a matter of fact, I can," said Barry. "One thing that's been worrying me a lot is, what has become of the other Jap ships that old Keith-Frazer shot up for 'em?"

"Ye're quite sure there were some others?"

"Positive. From what I was able to overhear, they had a battleship, a carrier and two light cruisers smashed up almost as badly as the *Tsushima*. What I want to know is, why haven't they brought 'em in here for repairs?"

"Probably because they chose to go somewhere else."

"Ah! But where else?"

Mr. Glencannon waved his hand. "I canna say exoctly — pairhops aroond to the Gulf o' Siam or to one o' their captured Dutch bases, for instance."

"Un-unh! They're all too far. Way, way too far. And so is every other base you can name."

"Aye? Weel, then, isn't it possible that they started to come here, but either sunk or got sunk on the way?"

"M'm, yes, it's possible — but, well," Barry shook his head, "it just didn't happen that way, that's all. If it had, we'd surely know about it. Even though they didn't tell us, even though we didn't hear them discussing it, we could read it in their faces, feel it in the air. Why man, if this morning's little shindig could upset 'em as much as it has, just think what a disaster like losing a battle wagon, a flat-top and two cruisers would do to 'em!" He stood up and went to pacing the floor. "No — I just can't figure it out," he muttered.

"Aye, weel, it does seem a wee bit perplexing," agreed Mr. Glencannon. "After all, four great fighting ships canna vanish into thin air, lik' so much evoporated whusky. And speaking o' that, Tommy," he milked the last drop from the bottle and tossed it out of the window, "— just reach into yon closet as ye gallop by, and snotch me oot a replacement, will ye? Er, as I say, four ships o' that size cudna. . . . Why, what's the matter, Tommy? What in the world have ye found, lad?"

Commander Barry was standing as though spellbound in the closet door, a bottle of Duggan's in one hand and a small, canvas-bound book held open in the other. On his face was a look of utter amazement.

"Sh-h-h!" and even though the dictaphone was no longer there, he glanced furtively toward the dresser as he hurried across the room. "Here, look!" he whispered, holding the book so that Mr. Glencannon could see the title page. "— Oh, boy; oh, boy! What do you know about this?"

"Nowt whatsoever," said Mr. Glencannon, frowning at the lines of Japanese print and at the same time relieving Barry of the bottle. "It looks lik' just so many mouse tracks to me. What in the world does it say, Tommy?"

Barry's voice was vibrant with excitement as he translated the book's title, "A *Special Extract From Secret Signal Code Number Four of the Imperial Nipponese Navy, Prepared for the Use of Members of the Naval Intelligence Service!*"

6

M r. Glencannon shrugged and proceeded to remove the seals from the bottle cap. "Ah, indeed?" he said, but it was plain that he was not particularly impressed. "Where did ye find it, Tommy?"

"Inside that open whisky case. I reached in under the top board for a bottle and felt something wedged way back in the far corner. I pulled it out and. . . ."

"Ho, dom!" blurted Mr. Glencannon. "That means there are at least two bottles missing! Why, the swundling scoondrel gave me a short measure!" He hastened to the closet, kicked the top boards from the other cases and peered eagerly within. "Nowt but whusky, thonk heaven!" he announced. "Swith, Tommy — for a minute, ye had me worried!"

"Where did you get that whisky, Colin?"

"From a half-caste Bengali by the name o' Mookerjee. Come to think o' it, I noticed at the time that one case had a loose board. Evidently the dishonest fellow had just then been stowing the book inside."

"Yes — or just breaking it out to use with a short-wave radio! Well, I s'pose Pandalang was lousy with spies, saboteurs and all the usual Jap fifth-column mob. No doubt your double-crossing half-caste friend is now sitting at home counting his thirty pieces of silver."

Mr. Glencannon leaned over to the window and looked out toward the ruins of the Bund quarter. Only with the greatest difficulty was he able to distinguish the remains of Clive Street in the blackened waste. "A-weel," he said, "the last I saw o' Muster Emanuel Mookerjee, he was heading for the cellar o' his estoblishment — and from the flattened-oot condition o' the place richt noo, I'm inclined to think he's still doon there."

"Hm'ph! So much the better." Commander Barry planted his elbows on the table, rested his head between his hands and concentrated his attention upon the book. From time to time he muttered exclamations of satisfaction or surprise. At length, Mr. Glencannon, watching him over the rim of his glass, was unable to restrain his curiosity.

"Why dinna ye read me some o' the exciting parts?" he asked, "— that is, if there's nowt off-color aboot them."

"Don't worry, this book is all strictly business! Boy, how I wish there was some way to get it to our people! Of course it isn't the full No. 4 Navy Code by a long shot, but it's got their complete system of identification and recognition signals and a flock of other vital stuff. Jeepus, what a find!"

Mr. Glencannon reached across the table and dragged the book toward him. It was heavy — so heavy that he realized there must be sheets of lead within the canvas covers, to sink it the instant it should be dropped overboard. Each page was divided into two columns, one of which contained Japanese text set in small type, while the other was filled with lines of conventional telegraphic dots and dashes. "A-weel," he said, scowling at it, "I've no doot it's all vurra interesting reading to anyone who can read it and is interested. But noo that ye've browsed yere way through it, Tommy, let's remove the lead, tear the rest o' it to pieces and get rid o' the dom thing doon the bathroom drain withoot a moment's delay."

"Get rid of it?" Barry stared at him incredulously. "Great guns, man, it's priceless! Why should we want to get rid of it before I've had a chance to study it?"

"Because it will do ye no guid to study it. Ye haven't got a radio, a blinker lamp, a semaphore or e'en a pocket flashlight to send a signal with — and ye haven't got anybody to send the signal to if ye did have. No, lad — I dinna relish the idea o' getting shot for not being an admiral, but I'll be domned if I'll get shot for having a book I dinna want and canna even read!"

"Well, now, hold your horses." Barry chided him. "I know as well as you do that if the Japs catch us with this book it'll be just too bad. And I know there's no sense tearing out the pages and trying to hide them in our shoes, or copying the code on cigarette paper, or any of that old movie boloney, either. Sure we've got to get rid of the book — we will get rid of it — but not until I've memorized every last word of it I'm able to cram into my head!"

Mr. Glencannon glanced once more at the dizzying scramble of mouse tracks and dots and dashes on the printed page before him, and shoved the book back across the table. "Foosh, lad!" he scoffed. "If ye think ye can memorize e'en enough o' that code to enable ye to buy drinks for the house in a Glasgow pub, ye're barmy!"

"Well, maybe I am," Barry admitted. "Still, by gosh, I'm going to try!"

For the remainder of the afternoon he sat poring over the book, tapping out dots and dashes on the table top and shaking his head. Evidently the going was tough. In contrast, Mr. Glencannon, who was doing some pouring of his own, made such phenomenal progress that he was obliged to start work on a new bottle.

When clinking sounds from the corridor warned of Nogi's arrival with dinner, Barry thrust the book under the cushion of his chair and sat back in scowling silence while the table was being set. Throughout the meal he responded to Mr. Glencannon's sallies of wit and humor only with preoccupied grunts. As soon as they were alone again, he resumed his studies, his grunting, his muttering and his tapping of dots and dashes.

"Ah, whoosh, lad, ye mak' me nervous!" complained Mr. Glencannon, fidgeting in his chair. "Ye remind me o' the time in the Balquhidder Assizes when my uncle, the late Reeverend Strathallan Glencannon, o' Craigellachie-on-Spey, was had up for sheep steeling. A mon o' pious works but with a weakness for alcohol, he was stonding there in the prisoner's docket, twuddling with the chain between his hondcuffs, while His Lordship was hemming and hawing and clearing his throat preparatory to pronouncing the sentence. Oh, ye can believe me, it was a vurra tense moment! But richt then, all o' a sudden, auld Uncle Strathallan speaks up and. . . ."

"Nuts to your Uncle Strathallan!" cried Barry, banging both fists on the table. "For Pete's sake, man — how do you expect me to memorize this stuff when you're spilling that kind of drivel?"

"I dinna expect ye to memorize it — that's exoctly the point! It's lik' the time another relative o' mine — Tamish Glencannon, a sort o' half cousin, he was, due to only one o' his parents being married — came doon to Drumlanrig from Ichnadamph to order himsel' a new truss. Weel, he was making the rounds o' the blacksmith shops and the iron mongers, getting bids on the job, when. . . ."

"Oh, good grief!" groaned Barry, pressing his hands against his temples and swaying back and forth. "Pipe down, pipe down, can't you?"

"Ah, swith, lad — I cud pipe up or doon or in any direction, if I only had my pipes!" said Mr. Glencannon, wistfully. "There's one auld tune I'd lik' particularly to skirl for ye — a beautiful thing called the *Pilbaireachd Coghiegh nha Shie*. No bagpipes being available, I'll endeavor to sing it to ye. It's in Gaelic, o' course, and it goes, er. . . ."

"No! Please!" Barry restrained him, but only in the nick of time. With a sigh, he closed the code book, lit a cigarette and sat moodily blowing smoke toward the ceiling.

Mr. Glencannon, gratified at finally having someone to talk to, proceeded to describe in detail no fewer than four separate and distinct methods of outwitting coin-in-the-slot telephones, the least complicated of which consisted in introducing a corset steel into the slot with a downward pressure approximating the weight of a coin, dialing a wrong number and then demanding a refund. But of course, as he pointed out, ladies wearing corsets are few and hard to find in these effete times, and ravishing one of them of a corset steel was likely to be a delicate business involving the police. The general subject of the fair sex reminded him of a lady he had once seen in a circus in Bilbao who had not cut her toenails for thirty-one years and was obliged to wear slippers made from inner tubes. By an easy transition, this brought him to the subject of three-toed sloths (Bradypodidae) and two-toed sloths (Choloepodinae) the difference between them being that while the former have three toes on each of their four feet, the latter have only two toes on the fore feet and three on the hind or two on the hind feet and three on the fore, he was unable to remember which. "— But in any case, I thought ye'd be interested in knowing aboot it," he said. "Ye see, Thomas, it has always been one o' my guiding prunciples to infoorm mysel' thoroughly in all conceivable motters, so ye mustna hesitate to call upon me for anything ye'd lik' to know. In a wurrd, my fund o' knowledge is exhaustive."

"Jeepus! I'll say it is!" Commander Barry spoke with deep feeling. "I should think it would exhaust you just to lug so much of it around! Why don't you go to bed, Colin, and get a little rest?" Commander Barry said.

"Aye, weel, wah-ho-hum!" Mr. Glencannon yawned. "— To tell ye the truth, I'm a wee bit bored, so pairhops I'd better." He drank one more tumblerful of whisky to sweeten his dreams and prevent them from fighting among themselves, then removed his clothes and lay down. "Yo-wah-hoo!" he yawned again. "Weel, guid nicht, Tommy, me lad! Dinna stay up too late wasting yere time with that book. There are sermons in stones and books in brooks and banks and braes o' bonny Doon where early falls the dew, a superior and most exceptional product, the un-vary-ing choice o' disc, dis, diz-z-z-z-z. . . ."

The snores assuring him beyond peradventure of a doubt that Mr. Glencannon was asleep, Barry heaved a sigh of relief and returned doggedly to work. But as well as he knew the Japanese language, with all its fearful intricacies, he found that trying to memorize condensations of whole sentences of it, translated into dots and dashes, was a well-nigh hopeless task. He knew what a handicap this archiac language was, even to the Japs themselves, in communicating modern, and particularly technical and scientific thought. But never until now had he realized what they were up against in coding for naval use a medium of expression suited to feudal warriors who wore two swords, painted pictures on silk with rat whisker brushes and made votive offerings to a volcano. And belatedly it occurred to him that no secret code, no matter what its basic language, could be simple enough to commit to memory — else why, in violation of the very fundament of secrecy, were all such codes set forth in print?

No, he couldn't memorize it — Glencannon had been right! Barry shook his head dispiritedly. It ached. "Hell!" he muttered, pushing the book away from him. He closed his eyes, but could not shut out the dots and dashes which flashed like fireworks across his tired retinas. Dully, he heard the sentry in the corridor singsong his orders to his relief, then slap a rifle sling as the new man saluted and took over. From Lord Wellesley Square, six stories below, came a rhythmic flutter of rubber soled feet and a snatch of birdlike chatter as the midnight patrol set out on its rounds.

"Well," Barry recalled himself with a start, "there's no sense putting it off! If I can't memorize the thing, the sooner I destroy it, the better!" He took up the book and strode resolutely toward the bathroom. Halfway there, he heard an eerie, droning sound, as though a squadron of dive bombers were peeling off and starting down. He halted, listened and realized that the sound came not from the sky, but from the general region of Mr. Glencannon's adenoids.

"Boy, is he hitting on all twelve!" he murmured, bending over the recumbent figure. "And look — just look at the hair on him! Wow! Why, I — I never saw anything like it in my life!" He bent lower to get a better view of the phenomenal thatch — and suddenly an idea came to him.

"Glencannon!" he whispered, shaking the sleeper by the shoulder. "Wake up, Glencannon!"

"A-z-m'm'm . . ." said Mr. Glencannon. "— Pairsonally, however, I always melt at least twenty per cent of bross into the mixture, whuch mak's the finished coin tinkle and ring lik' a genuine shilling. I — er . . . Eh? What's that?" He sat up. "— What's the motter, Tommy?"

Barry settled himself on the edge of the bed and waited until the other was fully awake. "Listen, Colin," he said, "have you ever come across any stories about the way the Egyptians and other ancient people used to send secret messages by tattooing them under the hair on the heads of slaves?"

"Haw, losh, many and many's the time, also Louis the Foorteenth!" said Mr. Glencannon brightly. "It always appealed to me as an ingenious though vurra brutal method. Er — " Abruptly he paused, rolled a fishy eye toward the code book on the bedspread and then licked his lips warily. "Er — o' course I can see what ye're driving at, lad — in fact, I'd thocht o' it mysel', but hesitated to suggest it to ye. Unfortunately, as ye can plainly see, the hair on my puir auld head is far too sparse to furnish odequate concealment, and thus the privilege o' being o' sairvice to my country is, alas, denied me. But as lang as ye insist, I'll be prood and hoppy to engross as much o' that code on yere ain scalp as there's room for — if ye can only think o' some way to do the tattooing!"

"Oh, I've got that part figured out," Barry assured him. "The tattooing can be done with the pen and ink that are over there on the writing table. We can simply break one nib off the pen, d'you see, and sharpen a needle point on the remaining one by whetting it on a floor tile. But, shucks, Colin, there isn't room enough on my scalp or anybody else's scalp for all the parts of the code I've got to copy. And so — well. . . ."

Instinctively, Mr. Glencannon's hand sought his bosom. He leaned forward tensely. His lips moved, but no sound emerged, so he raised his eyebrows questioningly. By way of answering the question, Commander Barry leveled his forefinger at the lush, tangled center of the thicket.

"Eh? Ah, no! No — not that!" cried Mr. Glencannon, his voice cracking to falsetto. He cowered back against the pillow, his arms clutched protectingly across him. "The — the pain wud be frightful — unbearable — excruciating! Ah, please, please, Tommy — say ye dinna mean it, lad!"

"You're damn tootin' I mean it!" said Barry grimly. "If we ever get out of this jam alive, that code's got to go along with us, see? If you can think of any other way to take it with us, speak up! If you can't — well, get up and start sharpening that pen!"

Mr. Glencannon closed his eyes and sat for a moment breathing stertorously; then, with a hollow sound, half sob and half groan, he lurched across the room toward the writing table.

Commander Barry leafed slowly through the code book, marking certain paragraphs and turning down the corners of the pages. He rose, adjusted the reading light and plugged in two additional floor lamps. The bed took on the dazzling, sinister brightness peculiar to prize rings and operating tables. As he stood viewing it, Mr. Glencannon came staggering back from the outer shadows. In one hand he clutched an inkwell and a sharpened, one-nibbed pen. In the other was a comb and a virgin bottle of Duggan's Dew of Kirkintilloch. He deposited them upon the night table and wilted to the bed.

"England expects every mon to do his duty!" he croaked. "Ye may f-fire when ye're ready, Gridley!"

Throughout the endless ensuing hours, Commander Barry jabbed, dipped and sweated, then dipped and jabbed again. Mr. Glencannon lay, drank, writhed, drank, moaned, drank, cursed and resumed drinking. The skin of his chest — particularly the central portion of it, where a zipper had once become entangled in the shag and nearly flayed him alive — was of a toughness customarily encountered in the more callous species of rhinoceros, and only the lustiest thrusts could penetrate it. Perversely, however, the toughest areas to pierce were those most sensitive to pain. St. Sebastian's celebrated martyrdom by arrows became but a trivial titillation compared to Mr. Glencannon's ordeal by pen. Mercifully, consciousness fled.

Barry turned toward the window to rest his tired eyes and saw a flush come over the eastern sky; imperceptibly, it changed from salmon pink to the delicate blue of a robin's egg and lo, it was day. The sun climbed up from behind Government House; then a bugle sounded and a rising sun of bunting raced the real one to the top of the flagstaff. Time was getting short! He tightened his grip on the pen. Mr. Glencannon's chest twitched spasmodically, like the hide of a water buffalo tormented by gadflies. "'Hark, hark the lark!'" he chanted weakly. "Oh, that we two were maying, doon some stream in the soft Spring breeze — zeeze — ziz-z-z-z. . . ."

"Hold it, boy; hold it! It won't be long now!" Barry muttered encouragingly. He turned to the last page and jabbed the final paragraph. It was done! The pen dropped from his nerveless fingers. He fumbled for a cigarette. "Whew!" he breathed. "Jeepus, creepus, what a night!"

Very gently, he lifted the book from Mr. Glencannon's heaving midriff and tiptoed to the bathroom. He ripped off the binding and tore the pages into tiny scraps, which he sped upon their way to join the waters of Kulong Strait. With a razor blade he severed the stitches which secured the canvas cover to the lead plates of the binding and reduced the fabric to shreds. He bent the plates double, stepped to the window and measured the distance to the shell of a burned-out department store across the street.

Footsteps sounded in the hall. There was a muttered order, followed by the thump of rifle butts. Barry turned and threw the lead plates from the window. As they vanished into the ruins below, a key clicked in the lock.

7

The door was opened by Commander Kaminashi, who stood aside to admit a tall, slim and slightly over-elegant Eurasian civilian wearing a cream-colored shantung suit and a supercilious smile; for the rest, the pastel-green puggree around his khaki sun helmet matched his tie, handkerchief and socks; he was smoking a pale green King's size cigarette in a long, green jade holder and under his arm he carried a morocco attaché case of the same color.

"Mr. Rodnikov, this is the American," said Kaminashi, coming to the point without the usual bowing and scraping. "The other prisoner is over there on the bed."

"Ah, really? I was wondering what that was!" said Mr. Rodnikov, breaking off his scrutiny of Mr. Glencannon and nodding to Barry. He seated himself at the table, unfastened his attaché case and proceeded to run through a sheaf of papers. "M'm, let's see now," he murmured languidly. "Ah, here we are! Tsk, tsk! — In some ways, y'know, this whole affair is really damned amusing!"

Commander Kaminashi stiffened. "Oh, do you think so?" he said acidly; then, mindful of Barry's presence, he shifted to Japanese. "Permit me to observe that you have a most peculiar sense of humor, Mr. Rodnikov!"

"It is one of my most fortunate attributes," replied Rodnikov in the same language. "Without it, the sorry spectacle which you navy people have made of yourselves would undoubtedly bring me down with acute melancholia."

"Indeed?" Commander Kaminashi bared his buck teeth in a sneer. "Well, if you will condescend to bring your celebrated intellect to bear on those reports you have before you, I think you will find that this whole affair was the fault of the army."

Rodnikov shrugged and returned his attention to the papers. Throughout this colloquy, Barry had stood with his hands in his pockets, registering sullen uncomprehension, but not missing a word. Presently, Rodnikov sat back and lit another cigarette.

"Well, Kaminashi," he said, still in Japanese, "there is no doubt that the army tank people captured the monstrosity who is now snoring over there on the bed — nor that he was wearing a British admiral's uniform at the time. But, my dear fellow, was that any excuse for the late Admiral Togawa to make fools of the entire Nipponese nation by bragging to the world that we had Admiral Keith-Frazer a prisoner?"

"But our Intelligence had reported that Keith-Frazer was the only British admiral in Pandalang!"

"— 'Our' Intelligence? Pardon me, Kaminashi — you mean *Naval* Intelligence! Keith-Frazer wasn't in Pandalang at all — he was at sea, in command of the British fleet, smashing up some of our finest ships. Oh, what a mess! Why, according to Togawa's own report, the prisoner himself denied that he was an admiral. Denied it vehemently!"

"Ah, yes — but then this American liaison officer identified him! How do you explain that, Rodnikov?"

"Well, I'm not in your — brilliant Naval Intelligence, of course, but it occurs to me that one way of getting the explanation might be to ask him. Er — look here, Commander Barry," he dropped into English, "I wonder if you'd mind telling us just when you arrived in Pandalang?"

"I flew in about eight hours before you people took it."

"Then I imagine you didn't have a chance to get very well acquainted with Admiral Keith-Frazer, did you?"

"Why, no," said Barry, doing some quick thinking and hoping it would turn out all right. "As a matter of fact, I never even saw him until Admiral Togawa had me brought in to identify him."

"What? Oh, come, Commander — then how could you presume to identify him?"

"Simply because I knew that there was only one British admiral stationed at this base, and — well, I just naturally figured he couldn't be anybody else."

Commander Kaminashi brightened up. "There now! You see?" he cried triumphantly.

Mr. Rodnikov ignored the interruption. "But surely, Commander Barry — surely you don't mean to tell me you still think that the Hairy Ainu on the bed is Admiral Keith-Frazer, do you?"

"No, of course not! All I know about him is that his name's Glencannon, and that he's a British merchant-marine engineer. All he knows is that he got drunk the night of the battle — and when he woke up, you people called him Keith-Frazer and gave him an admiral's uniform."

"Ah! Well, I rather fancy that's about all any of us will ever know about this whole affair. This — *amusing* affair, didn't I call it, Kaminashi?"

"You did!" replied Kaminashi angrily in Japanese. "But if you call this present farce an investigation — well, Rodnikov, I'm not satisfied and I'll take it to higher quarters! What was that fellow doing in the admiral's car, for instance?"

"'Keep your kimono on, little man!' 'Do not uncover the teapot and release the typhoon!'" Rodnikov quoted two ancient Japanese proverbs. "In

other words, my dear Kaminashi, don't be such a fool
as to go stirring this thing up any further. Remember what happened to Admiral Togawa! Remember
what happened to Colonel Shimoku! And above all,
please remember that you were Togawa's aide, and
therefore up to your neck in the whole shameful
business yourself!"

Commander Kaminashi was silent for a moment, and now his buck teeth were engaged in biting
his lower lip. Then, very slowly, he nodded. "I see
what you mean," he said. "Yes, Rodnikov, you are
absolutely right! What are your recommendations?"

"That the case be closed, hushed up, forgotten, and that the prisoners be sent to the concentration camp immediately, where you should have
sent them in the first place." He turned to Barry
and addressed him in English, "Commander, I'll have
to ask you to take off your things for just a minute,
while I make a search. Your friend Glencannon, as
I cannot avoid observing, is already in his natural
pelt and unable to conceal much besides scorpions,
ticks and perhaps a few quail. Got any luggage or
personal belongings, commander?"

"Only the toilet things Admiral Togawa sent
up to us. Oh, and Glencannon's got some whiskey
there in the closet. Say, what's this all about?"

"We're shifting you out to Victoria Point,
with the, er, less privileged prisoners. The whisky,
of course, cannot go with you."

The bed creaked. "No? Who says it can't?"
demanded Mr. Glencannon, rearing up in the full

glory of his shag and focusing his scowl on Mr. Rodnikov. "I dinna ken just who ye think ye are, sir, but whoever ye think ye are, I tell ye to yere face that ye're not!"

"No? My, my — how jolly awkward for me if you're right!" murmured Mr. Rodnikov. "Have you any other thoughts you'd care to develop, Mr. Glencannon?"

"Aye! As for yere ridiculous statement that my whusky canna accompany me, I call yere attention to Article Eleventy-three o' the Geneva Convention for the Humane Treatment o' Prisoners o' War, whuch states specifically, and I quote. . . ."

"Oh, save your breath — or at least don't point it this way!" Mr. Rodnikov interrupted him.

"Eh?" Mr. Glencannon's brows beetled. "What's that?" He lowered his feet from the bed and located the floor in almost the exact direction he had anticipated it. "Weel, noo, just let me warn ye, sir, that I resent yere thinly veiled insinuation that I smell o' spurp, spir-urp, spiritous liquors!" he declared. "Oh, ye may be able to hurl such slonders into the teeth o' some people with impunity, but there are other people at whom ye may not hurl such sonders into impuniteeth with the tune of! And I, sir," he raised his right hand dramatically, "—I, urp!, am one!" He brought down his fist in a sweeping gesture and smote himself resoundingly upon the chest. Simultaneously, a twinge of fearful agony assailed him, as though he had been stabbed. He emitted an ear-piercing scream and sprang to his feet. "Fiend!" he shrieked. "Ossossin!" Wild-eyed and gasping, he stumbled across the room, both hands groping on his tortured bosom for the hilt of the poniard that had pierced him. "Quick! Save yersel', Tommy!" he croaked. "He's — he's a knife thrower and — he's got me!" He fell into the closet and slammed the door behind him.

For a moment there was silence, then the sound of a bottle being opened, followed by protracted glugging. "Alas, Glencannon!" the voice came faintly through the panels, "To think that ye shud end up in agony in the dark — murdered, abondoned, licking yere wounds lik' some puir, stricken beast!" There was a salvo of sobs, more glugging and finally a heart-rending farewell, addressed to a friend named Donald Ferguson, Alex Ogilvie, Jock MacClontoch and, at times, Ramsey Calhoun, in the course of which he handed over his watch for delivery to his parents in Scotland and prudently demanded a receipt. The valedictory soared to notable heights, faltered, turned into a sepulchral moan and subsided in a snore.

Mr. Rodnikov nodded toward the closet door. "So! I fancy our friend has dropped out of circulation for a while." He took up Barry's uniform, examined the contents of the pockets, then turned the garments inside out and inspected the seams minutely. "— Well, everything seems to be in order, Commander; now I'll just have a look at Sleeping Beauty's drinking clothes. H'm! Nothing in the pockets, nothing up the sleeves. Oh, I say, though!"

He unbuttoned the heavily gold-braided shoulder boards from the admiral's jacket and held them up admiringly. "These are rather handsome souvenirs, what? Fifine da Silva can wear them in her adagio number in the floor show — though please don't ask me what she'll fasten 'em to! And the cap badge and these rows of pretty service ribbons — ha-ha!, why, they'll make a whole new costume for Koi-beto What's-Her-Name, that cute little dish on the end! Eh? Oh, yes, yes, Kaminashi, that'll be all!" he recalled himself to business. "Bring in your men and take custody of the prisoners, Kaminashi — I'll arrange about the special orders."

This time, they were taken out to Victoria Point in a humble, canvas-topped supply lorry, Commander Kaminashi riding in front with the driver, their guards sitting on captured cases of Lend-Lease tinned milk from Oneida County, New York, and themselves jolting around on the splintery wooden floor. Mr. Glencannon, groaning hollowly, fumbled alternately at his chest and at the region most vulnerable to splinters, while Barry listened to the sailors discussing the recent action at sea. All of them had served aboard the *Tsushima* and were as puzzled as he concerning the present whereabouts of the other damaged ships. When they fell to speculating on the matter, however, Kaminashi ordered them to shut up — not that he suspected Barry of understanding them, but merely because he considered it none of their business.

The concentration camp established to accommodate the several thousand European and Oriental prisoners taken at Pandalang was in the hot and dusty section of the dockyard formerly occupied by the garrison force of Royal Marine Light Infantry. It included the permanent barracks and mess halls and, in addition, streets of tents which had been newly pitched around three sides of the wide, sun-baked parade. The central space had been left open as an exercise ground for the prisoners. At intervals throughout the camp, floodlights were mounted on twenty-foot poles, while enclosing the entire area was a double fence of electrified barb wire commanded by a series of machine-gun towers.

"Well, it isn't a place you could just stroll out of absent-mindedly," Barry decided. "Wake up, Glencannon! Here we are!"

"No. Yes," said Mr. Glencannon, opening his eyes and promptly closing them again. "May it please yere lordship and the gentlemen o' the jury, I can only assure the court that when I purchased those three hoondred and twenty-six post cards in Port Said, I was under the impression that they were merely innocent scenic views o' that lovely city and its environs. Had I ever suspected, had I even so much as dreamed that. . . ."

The truck stopped at the headquarters barracks, the sailors vaulted out over the tailboard and one of them let it down with a bang. At the sound, Mr. Glencannon sprang to his feet and leaped to the ground as lightly as a gazelle. "Weel, weel, weel, it's the same quaint auld place!" he cried. "If only auld Pere Calomel is still presiding in the spotless *kitcheen*, as the French call it in French, I'll try to prevail upon her to stew us up an urp! sturp us up an ook! stew us up an octopus whuch, if ye've nere tasted it before, ye'll say is the finest sturped urptopook, pairdon me, stewed octopurp, ye've ever tasted, *n'est-ce-p'urp?*" A sailor prodded him with a rifle butt and herded him into the camp commandant's office with the others.

The commandant was a certain Major Mitsu, of the military police, originally a gangster, later a stool pigeon and eventually a captain of gendarmes in one of the more squalid precincts of the Yoshiwara, where his twin specialties had been extortion and torture. He was a stocky, pock-marked little brute, totally bald, and with one and one half ears missing; having nothing on which to hook his spectacles and no bridge in his simian nose on which to clamp a pince-nez, he wore a pair of horn-rimmed goggles secured by a pink silk ribbon passed around his head and tied at the back with a bow.

Commander Kominashi, who considered himself a *samurai*, made no effort to conceal his contempt for this vulgar army upstart. "Here," he said, tossing an envelope and a typewritten form on the major's desk, "Sign this receipt."

"Ah? More prisoners?" Major Mitsu leered up at the pair. "— One tough American and one drunken Briton, eh? Well, commander, I know exactly how to handle them!"

"You'll handle them exactly as directed in your orders!" snapped Kaminashi. "These men are useful to the navy — don't forget it!" He pocketed the receipt, beckoned to his sailors and hurried out, obviously relieved at being clear of the affair.

Major Mitsu looked after him sourly, then hoisted his feet to the desk top and proceeded to study his orders. A fly landed on his bald head; without shifting his attention from the papers, he caught it with a deft back-hand grab and slowly crushed it between finger and thumb. At length he nodded and glared at the prisoners through his goggles.

"I speak English," he announced. "— Barry, yess? — Grencarron, yess?" he pointed at each in turn. "— Okay! Orders say you both two must work for Nipponese Navy."

"Like hell we'll work for the Nipponese Navy!" cried Barry. "You know as well as we do that no prisoner can be forced to aid the enemy's war effort. Besides that, I'm an officer, and don't you forget it!"

"Oh?" Major Mitsu's lip curled in the regulation police manner. "Oh? So you thinking you are wise guy, eh?"

"Just try to make us work, and see what *you* think!"

The Jap lolled back, sucked his teeth and grinned insolently. "But maybe war last long time," he said. "Maybe last five year, maybe last ten year. If you no work, what can you doing all this long time, wise guy?"

"Don't worry, monkey — we'll just sit it out!"

"Aye — we'll sit it oot and ignore it!" Mr. Glencannon chimed in.

"Sit it out? Shish-shish-shish!" Mitsu turned in his chair and pointed through the window. "Come here, you both wise guys, and looking one moment at out there!"

Squinting into the heat waves which danced above the parade ground, they saw what appeared to be a lone, single-leafed plant which had managed to thrust its way up at the very center of the arid, hard-packed surface. A puff of breeze dispelled the dazzle and for an instant the leaf reflected the sunlight in a bluish metallic glint. They realized that it was not a growing thing, but a steel blade — a bayonet with its hilt set in a buried block of cement.

"You sit out war? Okay!" said Major Mitsu. "You like start sitting now?"

"N-n-no!" Mr. Glencannon was pale with horror. He gripped the window sill for support. "Braugh!" he shuddered. "I'm afraid ye'll have to excuse us. Ye see, I — I sat on some splinters on the way oot, and, weel, fronkly, I. . . ."

"Shish-shish-shish!" simpered Major Mitsu. "Oh, I think you agree is very more better to work for Nipponese Navy!"

"Well, yes, perhaps you're right," Barry conceded. "As a matter of fact, major, Glencannon and I have done a few odd jobs for your honorable navy already."

8

Major Mitsu called an orderly and bade him deliver the prisoners to Barrack Number Eighteen. As they followed him through the blazing heat of the camp streets, they were surprised to find the place as deserted as a suburban commuters' village on a week day. "Well, it looks like everybody's out working for the navy," said Barry. "That bayonet sure is the answer to the labor problem!"

"M'm!" said Mr. Glencannon, who had sobered up so suddenly that he had sprained his entire system. His chest felt as though a brush fire were raging on it.

Just inside the doorway of Number Eighteen, a guard was lolling on a canvas cot, studying pictures of duchesses in a tattered copy of *The Illustrated London News* and occasionally casting a supervisory glance toward a white-mustached old Englishman in underwear who was down on all fours scrubbing the floor. The Jap grunted at the new arrivals, pointed at two extra scrubbing brushes on a shelf and then at the Englishman's bucket. Just to make sure they knew what he meant and to convince them that he meant it, he took up a submachine gun from beside him on the cot, leveled it at each of them in turn and said, "*Ratta-tatta-tat!*" then, lighting a cigarette, he resumed his researches into *The Charitable Activities of Britain's Great Ladies in Wartime.*

"Nasty little beast, isn't he?" observed the old Englishman. "I say, you chaps'd better take off your uniforms before you start scrubbing — it plays hell with the drape of the trousers. My name's Birkett." They introduced themselves and shook hands. "I'm sort of housekeeper, charwoman and general drudge for this damn barrack while the guests are toiling in the yards," Mr. Birkett explained. "I fancy it's because I'm only a lowly banker, and not a gaudy technician like the rest of them."

"What's going on in the yards, anyway?" asked Barry.

"Why, the monkeys are literally stripping the place of equipment and shipping it home to Japan. They're shorthanded themselves, d'you see, so they're using our chaps for slave labor. Of course, most of

the prisoners in this camp are former civilian em-
ployees of the yards anyway — machinists, electri-
cians, shipfitters, riggers and what-not."

At noon, the whistle of the power station
blew; the guard bestirred himself, produced a mess
kit and some packaged rations from beneath his cot
and proceeded to eat his lunch. "We poor chamber-
maids are fed only twice a day, and filthy gunk it is.
My, my!" Mr. Birkett closed his eyes and smiled
wistfully. "When I think of my usual noontime
tuck-in of curry with rice, chicken, shrimps, Bombay
duck and all the rest of it — never less than fourteen different dishes — well, gentlemen, I, I. . . . "
His lip trembled and he turned away.

"Ho, foosh and for shame, sir!" Mr.
Glencannon addressed him sternly. "I fear ye're
nowt but a materialist! Dinna ye realize that there
are more important things in life than mere food to
stuff into yere belly? Why, richt this minute I'd
trade all the food in the world for a guid, stiff sowp
o' whusky!"

"Oh, but please, old boy! I'm not such a
materialist that I couldn't do with some whisky,
myself, or even a spot of gin!" said Mr. Birkitt,
defensively.

Throughout the afternoon they scrubbed, swept
and dusted. Mr. Glencannon thirsted and suffered
besides. At six o'clock the whistle sounded again,
and shortly thereafter long columns of weary prisoners
came shuffling into the camp. Nearly a hundred of
them, mostly Europeans, were quartered in Number

Eighteen. They sprawled on their cots, discussed the day's doings and cursed the Japs. The cursing was the sort that starts in the core of the soul and scorches its way outward. One man had been badly roughed up by the guards. "— But gor-blyme if I know why!" he said, plaintively. "There I was, just 'elping me mate to unbolt a drill press from the bed plates, when up steps this 'ere yellerbelly, takes me arm in a jiu-jitsu 'old and tosses me over 'is bleddy shoulder. I lands on the back of me 'ead, and while I'm laying there groggy, this other bloke jumps on me with both feet and goes fer a bit of a canter up and down me middle. Thank 'eavens, 'e 'ad rubber soles and not 'obnails!"

"Argh, the bleddy brutes!" said another. "This morning when we was loading them turret lathes aboard that ship the monkey 'oo was tending the winch deliberately let it run free and mashed two chaps from Number Two as flat as flounders. It was 'orrible — 'orrible!"

A bugle sounded and all hands filed across to the nearest mess barrack, from the door of which they were handed tin basins of rice and beans and cups of bitter tea. They ate in the open, squatting on the ground like coolies and fighting off ants and flies.

"Hey, stop scratching your chest," Barry whispered to Mr. Glencannon.

"But, I itch, dom it. I itch, I itch, I itch lik' the Barber o' Seville."

"I don't care who you itch like. Cut out the scratching before you get an infection and spoil that code."

"Foosh to the code! Anyway, I sterilized mysel' thoroughly when I was shut in the closet bidding fareweel to the whusky. — Ah, me!" Mr. Glencannon choked down a sob and what remained of his tea, and shuddered dismally as he thought of the future.

Next morning, the prisoners were routed out at dawn and assembled on the parade ground in full and impressive view of the bayonet. English-speaking sergeants called the roll and then, when necessary, acted as interpreters for naval officers who divided the men into groups and assigned them to various tasks. Apparently, the special qualifications of the newcomers had been carefully reported, for Barry was placed in charge of a gang which was assembling a battery of dry dock pumps in one of the principal shops, while Mr. Glencannon was ordered to Victoria Cove to superintend repairs on the sabotaged engines of a number of captured British and Dutch cargo ships.

And so began a period of toil, humiliation and misery. For Barry, it was also a season of perplexity. He knew that the main pumps of Number Three Dry Dock had been only slightly damaged by the explosion — certainly not enough to require their replacement. He knew that these new pumps, if they were actually sent to Japan, could be loaded, knocked down, in one fifth the cargo space that they would require when they were set up. Why, then, were they being assembled? Mr. Glencannon knew only that he had the engines of some twenty-six ships to check and repair, and that the bayonet was waiting if he didn't do it thoroughly. He did it thoroughly.

They saw each other only at night, by which time they were usually too fagged to compare notes or discuss the war. But just to make certain that all the prisoners in the camp should know how the war was going, the Japs took keen delight in blaring out recordings of English and American news broadcasts over the dockyard loud-speaker system. Invariably, the news was bad. On one occasion, an Australian commentator announced that the Japanese aircraft carrier *Kedzo*, previously reported sunk or severely damaged in the early action south of Pandalang, had now been definitely identified as operating at sea. "Damn!" said Barry. "How do you figure that one?"

In due course, Mr. Glencannon's chest ceased to bother him, but for some reason his nerves became increasingly ragged. For nights on end he dreamed that he was swimming in a vat of whisky in the distillery of Messrs. Mackenzie Duggan & Co., in Kirkintilloch, Scotland, only to have the whisky turn to water and himself wake up, screaming in horror. "I wish I had a clue to the meaning o' it," he said. Then, for a time, he took to having nightly arguments with a cobra by the name of MacCrummon, which he accused of monopolizing more than a fair share of his cot. The other prisoners, disturbed by the noise, concluded that he was suffering from a rare form of long distance delirium tremens. Finally, one night, the argument soared to unprecedented heights of violence; there were oaths and horrid sounds in the darkness; then, suddenly, all was still. They called to him, got no response and feared that the end had come. In the morning, however, they found Mr. Glencannon slumbering peacefully. A five foot cobra, very dead, was tied in a workmanlike sailor's knot around the leg of the cot. "When I pulled him up tight, he resented it bitterly," Mr. Glencannon explained. "I dinna ken why it is, but I've never been able to get alang with cobras named MacCrummon."

Every day, ships laden with machine tools, cranes, electrical equipment, steel plates and countless tons of other booty plowed out of Victoria Cove and headed eastward down the strait. Usually they were manned by their original Dutch or British crews, the only Japs aboard being three or four officers and an armed guard to control the captives. Sometimes several hundred prisoner technicians were crowded into the holds, presumably to install and operate the machinery upon its arrival in Japan. For these men, the future was not pleasant to contemplate.

Among the ships that had been more seriously sabotaged by their engineers was the *Amersdijk*, of Rotterdam; indeed, they made so good a job of it that the Japs lashed the four of them face to face around a sack of coal and shoved them overboard in a cluster. On the afternoon Mr. Glencannon finished the repairs and steam was ordered in the boilers, the last of Barry's pumps was just being hoisted aboard.

"A-weel, Tommy, me lad — what do ye suppose they'll set ye to doing the noo?" he asked, wiping his hands on a piece of oily waste and joining the naval officer on deck.

Commander Barry watched the bulky crate disappear down the hatch and chuckled mirthlessly. "Can't you guess?"

"Eh? Ah, swith, lad! Ye dinna mean that ye're — ye're?. . . ."

"Sure I do! They're shipping me away with the pumps — me and a hundred and twenty men. I got the orders this morning."

"Ho, dom!" said Mr. Glencannon. "I had a hunch it wud turn oot lik' that! Tsk! Tsk! Tsk!" He was silent for a moment while he bit a mouthful of bristles from the fringe of his walrus mustache and spat them thoughtfully over the side. "Weel, o' course I'll be vurra sorry to lose yere company, Thomas, but Jopon is a nosty hole and I canna say I envy ye the trip. I dinna mean to sound discouraging, but if by some miracle ye escape getting torpedoed and drooned on the way, it will only be a motter o' time before ye're either tortured to death or bombed to bits after ye get there. — Br'h!"

"Yes, it's a pretty grim prospect," Barry agreed. "How lucky it is that we're both facing it with our eyes open!"

"Eh!" Mr. Glencannon's knees went weak. "— *Both?*"

"Yop! You and I! The old team! Oh, I knew you'd be tickled when you heard the news, Colin!"

"Tickled? Tickled, foosh!" fumed Mr. Glencannon. "Oh, dom and blost the ungrateful yellowbellied scoondrels! Why shud they send I, me, mysel', who are so useful to them here, away on a perilous trip lik' this?"

"Because I asked them to," said Barry placidly.

"— Y-y-y-YOU?"

"Yes, sure! You see, for some reason, the Japs attach hell's own importance to these pumps of mine, so when I said I wanted to take you along to help me install'em — why, they agreed without the slightest hesitation. — Incidentally, you're chief engineer of this ship for the voyage so you won't have to sleep in the hold."

Mr. Glencannon turned red, then mauve, then purple. His knuckles cracked, so tightly did he grip the rail. A flood of indignation surged up from the uttermost crannies of his gizzard, but the only sound he could force from his lips was a feeble peep, like the whistle of an old maid's teapot.

"Oh, come, now!" Barry chided him. "Don't let yourself get into a lather, Colin! You certainly didn't think I'd go away and leave the code behind, did you?"

"The code?" Mr. Glencannon found his voice. "Oh, horns o' the devil — so the code's all ye want o' me, is it? The code — just the code! For a moment, at least, I gave ye credit for acting through friendship, however misguided! Pooh! I shud have known better, ye hoof-hearted Yonkee ghoul!"

Barry was about to placate him with soothing words when a stout old Dutchman with apple cheeks and Delft-blue eyes came up to them and bowed. "Goot afternoon, gentlemen," he said. "I am Captain Van der Zaan, master of this ship — subject, of course, to the orders of the *Japansche* very young snot who in command has been put. Which of you gentlemen is to be my chief engineer?"

"Mr. Glencannon is," said Barry, and then introduced himself. "When are we shoving off, captain?"

"When so soon we have steam. Mr. Glencannon, you will have as your assistants my head fireman and donkeyman. My formerly engineers were all by the *Japansche* barbarians most horribly gedrounded."

"Aye?" said Mr. Glencannon sullenly. "Weel, ye mustna be surprised if all yere new ones are horribly gedroonded likewise, before this trip is ower!"

"Yes, this is indeed a most likely," Captain Van der Zaan agreed. "— especially since I will not be permitted to navigate the ship or even to seeing a chart. The *Japanishe* very young snot, who is new from the naval school, will alone to navigate us. He has stolen my chronometers both, also my fine new

English Hezzanith micrometer sextant and may the rice in his dinner take root in his guts!"

"Aye, also the coconuts!" said Mr. Glencannon. "— But not before he gets us to Jopon."

Captain Van der Zaan shook his head and puffed out his apple cheeks. "If that even he can find Japan is for what I am vorry!" he said.

Two petty officers and thirty sailors came aboard, the latter lugging sea bags and tommy guns. Some of the men were posted at points of vantage topside and others were stationed in the engine room and stokehold. Four of them squatted around the coaming of number two hatch, below which Barry's hundred and twenty technicians were imprisoned in the hold.

The *Amersdijk*'s exhaust blew off with a roar; a jet of steam went rushing fiercely skyward, billowed out into a soft white cloud like the lather on a shaving brush and then condensed into raindrops which sprinkled to the deck in a lukewarm shower. A Dutch quartermaster came down from the lower bridge, touched his cap to Captain Van der Zaan, and addressed him in the language of the Netherlands.

"Well, the *Japansche* very young snot has giving the orders to sail," the captain announced. "Mr. Glencannon, you will now please to go below and take charge of the engine room."

"Yes, sir — and in view o' what we're in for, there's no place I'd rather be. People laugh at the ostrich for burying his head in the sand, but nobody ever heard o' an ostrich having a nairvous breakdoon."

All that afternoon the *Amersdijk* steamed down Kulong Strait, at times standing in so close to shore that the white bungalows of the rubber plantations were plainly visible through the trees. Seaplanes and mine sweepers were patrolling constantly, and more than once the vessel slowed down to follow pilot boats which guided her through narrow, zigzag channels across mine fields. Just at sunset, she passed Point Mallah on the starboard beam and by moonrise commenced butting her snout into the slow, majestic swell of the open sea. Next morning she was out of sight of land, a solitary speck on a sunny, gently heaving expanse of blue water.

Having assured himself by a cautious inspection through a porthole that no signs of war were visible, Mr. Glencannon emerged upon deck and joined Barry and Captain Van der Zaan.

"Guid morning, gentlemen!" he greeted them, endeavoring to impart a note of cheer to his voice. "Weel, here we are still alive — for whuch I suppose we can be thonkful, though no vurra. Captain Van der Zaan, pray forgive me if I obsairve that the auldfashioned cork lifebelts ye furnish on this ship mak' dom lumpy pajamas."

"Ach, so? I have never tried sleeping in one. Truth to tell, I have not sleeping at all last night, so much do I vorry."

"Oh!" Mr. Glencannon's bright smile wilted perceptibly at the corners. "— Indeed! Exoctly what were ye worriting aboot, sir — I mean in addition to worriting aboot everything?"

"I vorry about where we are going and whether if we get there! I vorry about whether we hit a reef! Three times in the night the *Japansches* have sharply changed the course."

"Aye, I thocht I heard the steering engine." Mr. Glencannon turned and glanced up at the sun. "H'm — weel — I'm no Ferdinand MacGellan or Marc O'Polo when it comes to novigation, but it doesn't look to me as though we're heading for Jopon."

"We're not — unless it's dragged its anchors and drifted down to Antarctica," said Barry. "That's just what's got the captain worried. As far as he can figure, we aren't heading for anyplace."

"No — I can think of no land to the south. Of course I do not know these waters — but also, I am certain, do not the *Japansche* young snot and his colleagues."

Presently, one of the latter came down from the bridge and ordered the bos'n to have the prisoners paint two Dutch and two Japanese flags on spare tarpaulin hatch covers — these, obviously, to identify the ship as friendly to aircraft of any nationality that might happen along.

"A-weel, that means that wherever we're going, they expect to meet planes on the way," Mr. Glencannon remarked.

"Then they must think Admiral Byrd's still doing business at the South Pole," said Barry. Say, wait — I just happened to think of something! The radioman hasn't gone to the bridge to get or deliver a single message since we left port. That means we're running blacked out."

"Yes, completely," agreed Captain Van der Zaan. "We are deaf and dumb as well as blind."

"— And never a drap to drink," added Mr. Glencannon, rounding out the line. "Tennyson wrote it."

At noon, the little Jap lieutenant and three of his subordinates lined up in the bridge wing with sextants and shot the sun, each noting down his results on a slip of paper. The officer compared the slips and nodded approvingly.

"Well, they seem to agree on the position, anyway," Barry grunted.

"That's undootedly because they've all made the same error," said Mr. Glencannon gloomily. "O' course, the mothemotical odds are exoctly sixteen mullion, two thousand, eight hoonderd and forty-four to one against it, or rather greater, but we must not underrate these Joponese."

"Oh, how I would that I could look at a chart!" said Captain Van der Zaan, gazing wistfully up at the chartroom. A sentry was sitting on a camp stool in the doorway, his tommy gun resting on his lap. . . .

Day after day, the *Amersdijk* plodded southward across the trackless ocean. Just under the surface ahead of her tumbling bow wave, dolphins aglow with jewels and flame flushed up schools of flying fish which swooped like swallows and skittered like rats across the hills and valleys of the swell. Whales lay basking luxuriously in the sunshine while families of terns and shearwaters perched upon their backs and dined on barnacles and seaweed; when the whales spouted, the birds would rise, screaming petulantly, circle about until the mist had cleared and then return to their meal. Manta rays as big as fighter planes leaped ponderously into the air and flopped back to the surface with splashes that could be seen and heard for miles. Once, they passed through a herd of dugongs — hairless tropic seals as smooth and pink as mermaids — at which the Japanese sailors shouted obscene remarks.

Then, one morning, the lookout aloft blew his whistle and pointed excitedly at a black dot moving across the cloud flecked sky far away on the port beam. At an order from the bridge, the guards commenced driving the prisoner technicians down the ladders into number two hold, while Jap sailors stood ready at the hatches of one and four to unfurl whichever of the painted tarpaulin covers, Dutch or Japanese, might prove to be appropriate.

The black dot wheeled slowly around the edge of a cloud and headed for the ship, coming down on a long slant. They heard a droning sound, louder than the hum of the wind through the stays. Mr. Glencannon licked his lips and retracted his head between his shoulders, like a turtle getting ready to retire within its shell. "H'm, a-weel," he said, with elaborate casualness. "if ye'll pairdon me, Tommy, I think I'll just step below for a moment."

"If you'll pardon me, I think you'll just step into this doorway!" said Barry, dragging him by the arm. "Lively, man — those monkeys'll start signaling in a minute! Unbutton your jacket and hold it open — so! — and take this comb. Stand facing me, so I can look out over your shoulder. When I say *go!*, start combing yourself upwards — slowly, very slowly, so I can read you. Get the idea?"

"Aye!" said Mr. Glencannon, trembling so violently that the hairs on his chest gave off a dry, rustling sound, like hay in a windswept meadow. "B-b-but suppose it's an Allied plane and starts b-bombing us, Tommy?"

"It isn't and it won't," snapped Barry. "It's a big four-motored Jap job — looks like a Hiro 97. Yes the Japs have recognized it now — they're spreading their Rising Suns on the hatches. Now the plane's dropping lower for a look-see. Wup — wait, wait. . ." There was a preliminary flicker from the blinker lamp in the plane's nose, then a series of flashes. "Go! Start combing!" Barry ordered, "*Da-da, de-da-de, de-d-d-d-d* . . ." His voice trailed off in a droning mumble as he read the dots and dashes. "They're using Code Number Four, all right! That signal's Number Thirty-three, I think — yes, now they're repeating it in the other form, spelling out the numerals — S . . . A . . . N; S . . . A . . . N. It means 'IDENTIFY.' Now there goes the blinker on the bridge! — Comb yourself slower, Colin — slower, dammit, slower!"

"I — OUCH! — am!" Mr. Glencannon winced violently as the comb jerked through a snarl and tore out a tuft that could have served him as a spare mustache.

For the next five minutes he combed his chest and suffered while Barry read as much as he could of the signals; then the great plane roared past at masthead height and put back on its course, the goggled gnomes aboard her waving farewell to the cheering Japs on the *Amersdijk.*

"Where did it come from and where is it going?" mused Barry, looking after it; then, turning to Mr. Glencannon. "Well, button your jacket," he ordered. "You're just about the unhandiest signal book I ever used!" But though some of the messages had eluded him, he felt that he had gained at least a working knowledge of the challenge and identification system embodied in Secret Code Number Four of the Imperial Nipponese Navy.

Later that day, Captain Van der Zaan called their attention to a cloud on the southern horizon; it was heavier and creamier than its neighbors and the shadows on its belly were perceptibly darker. "At this season is a cloud hanging around over every island. It never fails," he said. "I am certain it is an island under that one."

"M'm, yes, captain, I believe you're right," said Barry. "Look at that Jap up there on the bridge, getting busy with the pelorus. It must be an island, sure enough!"

"Yes, but what island? I can think of none within a thousand miles of where we must be."

"Search me! The first time I was ever south of Luzon in my life was the day I took off for Pandalang."

"Aye, and a trogic day it was for me," said Mr. Glencannon with emotion which came not only from his heart but from a number of other internal organs.

As the afternoon wore on, they watched the cloud apparently being pushed up over the curve of the world on the crest of a mountain peak; then lesser peaks reared slowly out of the sea, until presently they could see the whole green, steep-walled mass of an island. There were no houses, no signs of a harbor, and yet the *Amersdijk* bore steadily on. Steam was ordered in the winches and the Dutch crew set to work opening the hatches and unslinging the derricks.

"Well, there must be a break in it somewhere, but darned if I can see it," said Barry, scanning the tree-covered slopes. "Maybe it's around on the other side and . . . oh-oh! Here comes something!"

It was a motor torpedo boat and it was coming fast, bouncing and squattering over the long swell and throwing out sheets of spray which were tinged at the edges with the colors of the rainbow. While still some distance away she flashed a challenge with her blinker lamp, to which the *Amersdijk* responded. Making perhaps forty-five knots, the little craft cavorted in a circle around them, banking steeply; then she drew ahead and slowed down.

Barry was pleased to find that he could just get the gist of the signals without having to look them up on Mr. Glencannon. "She says she'll pilot us in," he announced. "Yop, and I think I've spotted the entrance now. — See that sort of shadow in the trees, as though a canyon comes down to the shore? And see that little stretch at the lower end of it where there isn't much surf?"

"Yes, yes, I think that there is the passage," agreed Captain Van der Zaan. "There must be a lagoon, a flooded crater, within the island. But we are now where is getting shallow — too damned shallow! Look!" He pointed over the side at masses of kelp and sea tangle which swayed back and forth as the surge swept over the scantily submerged rocks.

For a quarter of a mile they ran parallel to the coast, keeping just beyond the outer line of roaring, boiling surf. The torpedo boat doubled back sharply through a patch of deep, calm water. The *Amersdijk* swung around to follow, and there, revealed before them, was a crack, a gorge, a gateway, like the entrance to a fjord. It was narrow — perhaps no more than a hundred yards across — and so short that they could see the farther end of it. The sides rose vertically to about the level of the vessel's masthead and then sloped away in a widening V so high that the tops were lightly veiled by the misty lower strata of the clouds. As the ship nosed cautiously into this sheltered passage, they no

longer heard the breakers, but only the hiss of her
bow wave and the rumble of her engines echoed
back strangely from the towering walls.

In a matter of minutes they emerged upon a
broad glassy lake, its shores and the mountainsides
behind them deep green with trees and jungle growth.
It was like being at the bottom of a great jade bowl.
A flock of water fowl rose wheeling and screaming
at the vessel's approach, leaving the placid surface
flecked with white feathers; they circled for a moment, flapping slowly, then headed for the passage
and the open sea. There were no other signs of life
in all the lovely scene.

"Ah, swith!" said Mr. Glencannon, with re-
luctant admiration. "If only this place was someplace else and we had a cauld veal pie, it wud be an
ideal spot for a picnic, if only we had some whusky!"

But just then, abruptly, startlingly, there came
to them from across the lake the faint but unmistak-
able chatter of pneumatic rivet guns, and deep within
the tangle of foliage on the farther shore they saw
gushing cascades of sparks from oxyacetylene torches.

"Hell!" exclaimed Barry, pointing excitedly.
"There's a ship in there! A big one! All camou-
flaged!"

"Aye! — She's a battleship!" Mr. Glencannon
declared. "And if ye'll look alang a little farther to
the left, ye'll see at least one cruiser, and possibly
two, hidden under leaves and bronches."

"And to the right are still more ships, and
more — the kind I cannot tell because of the trees

lashed to them and the leaf-covered nettings," said Captain Van der Zaan. "Also is a steam dredger."

"Well!" Barry's voice was husky and he drew a long breath. "Well, gentlemen — now we know what the Japs did with the four ships that were too hard hit to make Pandalang! Now we know where they repaired the carrier *Kedzo* and got her back to sea! Now we know why they've sent us here, along with all the other shiploads of men and materials!" He moved to the rail and gazed wonderingly around the lake. "Boy, oh boy, what a hide-out! They've got a base here that's even better than Truk!"

With her engines rung down to DEAD SLOW, the *Amersdijk* ran in so close to shore that trees brushed her starboard lifeboats and vines snapped off in her rigging. The telegraph clanged for STOP; she lost way, and her anchor chains went *clunketty-clunking* down through the hawse pipes. As she came to rest, swaying gently in the swell of her own wake, she was made fast alongside a crude wharf, really a sort of loading platform which had been built by paving the bank with logs. Motor trucks piled with tree branches, netting and other camouflage material came bumping across this platform. A gang of coolies unloaded them, swarmed up the ladder and commenced blending the ship into the landscape.

On the *Amersdijk*'s bridge, the young Japanese lieutenant was relaxing with a cigarette. Plainly, he was feeling pleased with himself. He strolled to the rail, rested his elbows upon it and grinned down at the trio below. As far as they were aware, it was the first time he had deigned to notice them.

"Well, you dumb jerks had it all figured out I wasn't gonna make it, didn't ya?" he taunted in flawless Californian. "I guess old U.C.L.A. teaches a pretty good navigation course, at that — eh, Commander?"

"Good enough for bright young Nisei house boys to steal and take home to Japan with the spoons," said Barry, hoping to get a rise out of him. "By the way, Admiral Disiwashi — I wonder if you're bright enough to spell the name of this place?"

The Jap grinned. "Yeah, bud, I'm bright enough. I'm even bright enough not to!" He took a final drag on his cigarette, flipped it down into their midst and then spat after it.

Captain Van der Zaan clapped one hand to his cheek, blurted an oath and reached for his hip pocket. The Jap ducked into the chartroom doorway and fired two shots around the edge of it. The old man wilted to his knees, slumped forward on his face and lay twitching. There were three more shots, fired slowly, and the twitching ceased.

"There!" said the Jap, strutting back to the rail. "I guess that'll teach the crazy old Dutch tub of guts not to pull a gun on me!"

"It wasn't a gun," said Barry. "It was only a handkerchief. Here, look!"

"Oh!" The Jap seemed disappointed, even a trifle embarrassed. He crooked up his arm and shoved his pistol back into the shoulder holster. "Well," he said sullenly, "Maybe it'll teach the rest of you lugs to be a little more polite!"

The old man wilted to his knees, slumped forward on his face and lay twitching. There were three more shots, fired slowly, and the twitching ceased.

9

Close in to the wooded shore and hidden beneath a vast, shady bower of foliage, raffia and netting lay the 35,000-ton battleship *Hoshino*. Her decks were leaf-strewn, her guns festooned with vines, and in the trees secured to her tops and funnels, birds of brilliant plumage fluttered and screamed. The mighty gray fighting ship in that peaceful sylvan setting made a spectacle almost awesome in its strangeness, like something dreamed up out of absinthe and opium by a surrealist painter. She simply didn't belong there, and yet — there she was!

In the water around her torpedo-ripped stern and extending well forward along her port quarter was a cofferdam — a sort of double-walled stockade of square-faced piles driven into the lake bottom, the space between the walls filled with concrete. Within this enclosure, the surface of the water was seething and bubbling with air from the helmets of divers working below; outside it, a broad area of the lake was colored a milky gray by cement soaked from thousands of bags which other divers were piling under the *Hoshino*'s bilges to cradle her upright when the cofferdam should finally be emptied and her flotational stability disturbed. But though empty it would have to be before her damaged plates and propellers were exposed, the difficulties of pumping it out were enormous. To begin with, it was by no means watertight, especially where its ends met the sides of the ship, and there was constant seepage up through the gravel bottom. Then most of the available divers were ex-pearl fishermen, accustomed only to clear water and knowing nothing of heavy salvage work or the use of submarine power tools. Finally, the pumps had proved utterly inadequate to the task at hand. Experimental alterations had been made upon two of them, and now Commander Barry, Mr. Glencannon and a group of Japanese salvage officers stood leaning over the battleship's taffrail, anxiously watching the fall of the water level as revealed by gauge marks painted on the cofferdam piles.

"Shish-shish! I think that this time is working very, very better!" announced Captain Higashi, with considerable over-optimism.

"Yes, both units are now discharging most gratifyingly," agreed Lieutenant Okimoto, an earnest young naval constructor. He squinted at the gauge marks, clicked the release button of his stop watch and made some rapid but erroneous calculations with his slide rule.

"Shish-shish! Ish! Shish!" said naval constructor Lieutenant Nakagawa, expressing unreserved approval of the proceedings.

Just then, however, one of the pumps gave off a hollow, clanking sound, belched out approximately half a ton of rocks and stopped dead.

"Bang! That's done it!" cried Barry. "Oh, I told you it would happen! These things aren't stone crushers — they're pumps, designed for emptying dry docks and handling nothing heavier than silt. They're — wup! — BANG! There goes the other one!"

The Japs stood for a moment in stunned silence; then Captain Higashi, rising to his responsibility as senior salvage officer, waddled to the nearer pump and dealt it a furious kick with his Size 3 foot. "Oh, very damn you!" he reprimanded it shrilly. "Oh, stinking pump!"

Lieutenant Okimoto spread his hands in a gesture of helplessness. "Ah, but what in the world is to doing now?" he appealed to the American.

Barry shrugged disgustedly. "Well, I'm sick and tired of trying to salvage your tin navy for you, but when I tackle a job, I like to finish it. If the fools at Pandalang had only told me what these pumps were intended for, in the first place, I'd have put special filters in them and redesigned the intake heads. If you want me to take 'em back to Pandalang now and make a decent job of it, okay. If not — well, gentlemen, the lake is handy and you all know how to jump!"

The Japs nodded solemnly, then moved out of earshot and fell to chattering and chirping among themselves. Barry had Mr. Glencannon put a gang of mechanics to work opening up the pumps, and returned to the rail, where he stood looking moodily out upon the lake. In the center, great flocks of white sea birds were gathered as usual. Half a dozen single-float Zeros appeared from among the mangroves on the opposite shore, taxied in circles to warm up their motors and took off in formation; the birds rose, screaming, circled briefly, then settle down again to feed. A heavily laden tanker came plodding in from the pass and tied up astern of the cruisers; then a freighter in ballast backed out into the open and headed for the sea — bound, probably, for Pandalang or one of the Dutch or Chinese ports for another load of laborers and loot. From somewhere back in the hills came a dull *boom!* as gun emplacements were blasted out of rock, while in the woods nearer at hand, Diesel bulldozers coughed and clattered as they leveled the runways of the newly cleared airfield. It was a busy place, no doubt of that, and daily becoming busier.

Barry had been on the island for nearly a week, but it still seemed fantastic, incredible, impossible. Actually, he told himself, it was surprising. Now that he took time to reflect on the matter, he realized that Truk and many other Japanese bases in the Carolines, Marshalls and elsewhere would have seemed equally surprising, had he come upon them under similar circumstances. Those islands, too, were secret bases; they had remained secret for years, even though in peace time the sea and air were free and secrecy infinitely more difficult to maintain than at present. Inevitably, the war had exposed a few of them — but even today, what did anyone know of Truk, Ponapé, Saipan and the rest, except that they actually existed? And how many others, like this one, were still undreamed of?

Of course the Japs' chief concern here and now, was to repair the damaged ships and get them back to sea. Once that was accomplished, they could concentrate their efforts upon consolidating the position. They would mine the approaches, fortify the heights, install a powerful garrison; they would bring in squadrons of land-based fighters and bombers, and maintain a screen of submarine, surface and air patrols. The place, then, would be formidable. "Yes, and pretty darned near impregnable," mused Barry, looking around him. "Right now, their main protection is camouflage — radio silence — secrecy. We've got to figure some way to sock 'em before they really dig in and get set!"

Mr. Glencannon approached along the deck. "A-weel, Tommy-me-lad!" he chuckled. "I'm vurra hoppy to report that both o' yon pumps have literally chewed oot their ain insides and spewed them into the lake."

Barry glanced warily toward the conclave of chattering Japs. "Then there's no danger of anybody noticing that those lock nuts are missing?"

"Losh, no — there's so much else missing that mere lock nuts are merely mere! But tell me, Tommy — why did ye mak' that crazy suggestion aboot going back to Pandalang?"

"Because we've got to get away and spread the news about this place, that's why! I don't know how we'll do it — all I know is that we haven't got a chance as long as we stay here. But during a round trip to Pandalang — well, anything might happen!"

"Aye? What, for example?"

"Oh, lots of things — I dunno, exactly! We might chuck over a bottle with a message in it and. . . ."

"— And ten years from noo, a pickaninny in Australia micht find it on the beach and throw rocks at it. Foosh, ye talk lik' a gowk."

"All right, then, we might escape! Remember, we won't have those hundred and twenty prisoners along, so there probably won't be many guards. Why, shucks, Colin, we might even meet an Allied ship!"

"We micht even get sunk by one, ye mean!"

"Okay, so what? There'd be a good chance of her picking us up, wouldn't there?"

"Not if the sharks saw us feerst! No, please, Tommy — let's try to be sensible aboot this thing. If we. . . ."

"Pipe down!" Barry interrupted him. "Here come the Three Wise Monkeys with their decision."

"Commander Barry, I have deciding yes," announced Captain Higashi. "You and Mr. Glencannon must take all six pumps to Pandalang so very, very soon as we can put on ship and go. Lieutenant Okimoto and Lieutenant Nakagawa will going with you. Goo'bye."

"Goo'bye to you, Captain," and though Barry's fingers touched his visor in a salute, his thumb was pressed firmly to the end of his nose.

It was late that afternoon before Lieutenant Nakagawa, at the wheel of an American jeep, drove out on the landing stage alongside the *Hoshino* and beckoned Mr. Glencannon and Commander Barry to join him. "All pumps are now loaded," he announced proudly. "Oh, very quick job! Beat Englishman with whip, make hurry up. We sail tonight." Still simpering, he let the clutch in with a jerk and turned down the rutted road that ran along the lake front.

It was the first time the pair had been ashore since their arrival and they could not but marvel at the progress that had been made. Except for the ever-present camouflage and a certain inevitable crudeness, the place was beginning to look like what it might someday be — an extensive naval-repair base. Though most of the machine shops were still mere open sheds with corrugated roofs, all were in operation. Looking down the leafy side roads which prisoners were cutting through the woods, they saw barracks, tents and endless rows of huts in which the captives were quartered. Once, at the entrance to such a road, they were stopped by military police while a battery of medium howitzers clanked past them on its way into the hills.

On all sides there were signs and sounds of industry, and suddenly, if belatedly, it occurred to Barry to ask himself where the necessary power was coming from. Whence, for that matter, had come the electricity to operate the pumps and other machinery on the *Hoshino* salvage job? He guessed the answer even before he looked up into the trees and saw the thick black power cables that were strung from one to another of them. The cruisers!

Lieutenant Nakagawa followed the direction of his gaze and chuckled. "Yes, is very good idea, isn't?" he asked. "Idea first used by American Navy ten, twelve years ago at Tacoma, Washington. City power station then have busted, so aircraft carrier *Lexington* make all electricity for city, even streetcars. You know of?"

"Yes, I know," said Barry dryly, "— but I didn't think you did."

"Shish-shish-shish, oh, sure! Captain Higashi have go to Tacoma and study this matter for three months, then write book about. Look, please!" He pointed. "There are cruisers now."

Seen through their camouflage, the two ships appeared to be but little damaged, although the sound of rivet guns indicated that work was still in progress.

"Are almost fix," said Lieutenant Nakagawa. "Could go to sea now, if must have to, but are staying here to make electric power until machinery come from Nippon. Shish-shish! Yes, is a very good American idea, thank you so much!"

As they jolted along a stretch of water front occupied by a row of freighters, Barry noticed that Mr. Glencannon was leaning back with his eyes closed, sniffing the air. His first thought was that a grog shop must be somewhere in the offing, but when he realized that such could not be the case, he nudged the sniffer with his elbow. "Hey, stop it!" he said. "You're making a draught."

Mr. Glencannon ignored both the nudge and the admonition; indeed, he did not even open his eyes. "F'mf! F'mah!" he sniffed, and his face was suffused with a glow of ecstasy. "Beef bones from Rosario! Raw hides from Bonus Airs. Nitrates from Antofagasta! All packed doon there in the hot, hot holds, fuming and sweating and moldering together! Ah, losh — how delichtful, how entroncing, is that heavenly effluvium!"

At that moment Lieutenant Nakagawa brought the jeep alongside one of the freighters and slammed on the brakes. "Shish! Here our ship!" he announced.

Mr. Glencannon opened his eyes, gazed up at the vessel's rust-pitted side and smiled the smile of a pilgrim who sees the blessed hills and valleys of the Promised Land. "The *Inchcliffe Castle!*" he breathed reverently. "The fulthy, frowsty, rickety, rotten, dear auld *Inchcliffe Castle!* Phew! I knew dom weel she was aroond here somewhere!" Moving as though in a trance, he stepped from the jeep and followed the others up the splintery, shin-breaking ladder. Mr. Montgomery was standing on the upper grating.

"Hm'ph, so it's you!" the mate greeted the prodigal sourly. "So yer'v finally decided to come skulking back aboard and favor us with yere charming company, 'ave yer? Welp, I must say it's 'igh time! Where the 'ell 'ave yer been these past few months — off carousing and debauchering around all over Southeast Asia?"

"It's none o' yere dom business where I've been, so foosh to ye!" retorted Mr. Glencannon, his trancelike demeanor giving way to a lowering truculence. "Stond oot o' my way, ye puling cockney blipe, before I forget my breeding and speak my mind to ye!" He took a quick step forward, his walrus mustache bristling like a shoe brush.

"Ker-hem! Ker-Huff! Now, now, gentlemen, I mean to say!" Appearing in the nick of time, Captain Ball intruded his considerable bulk between them. "— I mean to say, er, that is — why, yes, yes, bless my soul if it isn't Mr. Glencannon! Well, well, well, how are you, Mr. Glencannon?"

"I'm vurra weel indeed, thonk ye kindly, Captain Ball. How are ye yersel', sir?"

"Oh, I suppose I can say I'm feeling fit — yes, quite fit, everything considered. Commander Barry? I'm honored to meet you, Commander Barry! Permit me to welcome you to my ship, sir — er, such as these yellow lice have left it, and as far as they'll let me! Why, would you believe it, sir," his fists clenched and he started trembling violently, "would you believe it, the — the little . . . !"

"Ush. 'Old 'ard, sir," whispered Mr. Montgomery, grasping him by the arm and grimacing warningly toward the bridge. "There's no sense 'aving it 'appen again. Come, now — is there, sir?"

"M'm, er, well — " Captain Ball wilted somewhat, but continued to tremble. Mr. Glencannon, studying him, noted with concern that his face had lost its accustomed ruddiness and turned gray and flaccid — that his paunch, once a proud, firm monument to Herfordshire beef, Yorkshire pudding and all that is British and best, had become but a bloated repository for Rangoon rice, Seoul soyas and similar mean fodder provided by Nature for her Asiatic millions whose bellies she has fashioned small and colored yellow. It was plain that the old gentleman had been having a rough time. . . .

The captain stopped trembling and licked his lips. "Mm, er, yes, you're quite right, Mr. Montgomery," he agreed weakly. "As you say, there's no sense in my kicking up a fuss and having more trouble with them. Oh, I don't know how to tell you about this, gentlemen — it's — it's too humiliating." He turned his head away. "Earlier this afternoon them two new navy monkeys had me — had me — flogged! Yes, gentlemen!" He faced them squarely and tried to blink back the bitter tears, "They actually had me flogged! — Me! — Flogged! Right here on my own ship, in front of my own crew!" He groaned and swayed back and forth in helpless anguish.

For a moment there was silence; then, "Ho, dom!" growled Mr. Glencannon in the depths of his throat. "So they did that to ye, did they? Weel, I'll just go up there and. . . ."

"Hold it, Colin — hold it!" Barry restrained him evenly. "You'll only get yourself shot if you start anything now. Later, maybe we can plan something."

"Hey, Captain Fat!" came a shrill voice from the bridge. "Wake up, you old Captain Fat, and let us getting started! You like maybe get your backside whip some more, you big, fat Englishman?"

Captain Ball looked up at Lieutenants Okimoto and Nakagawa, who were grinning like twin Cheshire cats over the weather cloth. "Very well, gentlemen," he said with great dignity. "I shall give the orders to cast off at once."

Presently, the *Inchcliffe Castle* swung clear of the shore and headed for the pass, whence a torpedo boat would guide her to the open sea. Barry stood looking back at the leafy masses which he knew were ships; they became vague, then merged into the green of the background and were gone. As the vessel neared the center of the lake, he watched the birds rise mewing and screaming, and thought that the white feathers they had left behind looked like lillies in a pond. He wondered what the birds had been feeding on, and suddenly he knew. For now it was as though the *Inchcliffe Caste* were plowing through a sea of corpses. There were tens, dozens, perhaps scores of them. As they bumped soggily against the side or sea-sawed and tumbled in the swell, he saw white men, Filipinos, Chinese, Malays and many about whom there was no telling. He turned away. From the wing of the bridge, Lieutenants Nakagawa and Okimoto looked down at him and waved. "Shish-shish-shish!" they simpered in unison.

The following night when the moon came up, the *Inchcliffe Castle* was patiently unrolling her straight white wake like a carpet on the surface of the sea. It was calm; the only sounds were the swish and slap of water against the bows, the dull rumble of the engines and occasional footfalls and snatches of sing-song chatter from the Japs on the bridge. Half of the eighteen guards were at their stations at various parts of the ship; the other nine were sleeping in the port side of the forecastle formerly occupied by the *Inchcliffe*'s black gang. The latter were now quartered in the starboard side, doubled up with the deck crew.

Barry, Captain Ball and Mr. Montgomery were sitting on the forward hatch, looking at the moon and conversing in cautious undertones.

"Why, there's hundreds of men know about that island, and have for years," Captain Ball was saying. "Kampan is the name of it — it's even shown on some of the charts. The chap who told me said that there wasn't any lake in it till 1923, when the tail end of the earthquake that hit Japan must've opened that crack in the wall and let the sea in. He said he reported it to the Admiralty in Australia and later on in London, but they just looked down their genuwine Chippendale noses at him and said, 'Oh, relly? How veddy, veddy odd!' Meanwhile, the Jap pearl poachers had took the news to Tokyo, where people still wear brains."

"Well, the trouble ain't that they're so smart; it's that we're so stupid," said Mr. Montgomery. "Why our ruddy navies and air forces 'aven't yet got wind of that base is wot beats me!"

"Well, ga-huff, the way they're running this war, the whole mess is nothing more nor less than a holy mess!" declared Captain Ball, shaking his head. "Why, just take the way they wouldn't give me my orders to clear out of Pandalang until it was too late. I'd no more than sounded the whistle to warn Glencannon when the monkeys came swarming aboard and caught us with our sarongs down."

"Haw! Speaking o' the devil, here I am!" Mr. Glencannon's voice came from the shadow of the forecastle. It had a peculiar flat and toneless quality, as though the vocal cords were coated with molasses. He stepped into the silvery moonlight beside the hatch, cleared his throat lustily and stood swaying in a manner certainly not attributable to the gentle motion of the ship.

"Urg!" he said. He raised his eyebrows in a puzzled fashion and turned to Mr. Montgomery. "Did ye just noo say 'urg'?" he demanded.

"No, you did."

"Did I? Strange! I was trying to say *urp!*"

Barry seized him by the shoulder and sat him down on the hatch with a thud. "Drunk! Yes, drunk, by gosh!" he whispered fiercely. "Well, you're a fine mess, I must say. Don't you realize we're in a spot where we've got to keep our wits about us? Can't you see we've got to be on our toes every second, so that when our chance comes, we'll be all ready to — to. . . ."

"To kill the Jops and seize the ship? Aye!" and now Mr. Glencannon's voice blared out like a foghorn. "It's precisely aboot that, precisely, that I was aboot to tell ye aboot! Ye see, Tommy-me-lad. . . ."

Barry clapped his hand over the other's mouth. "Shut up, you chump!" he hissed. "Do you want to get us shot? Don't you know there're at least nine Japs inside that fo'c's'le door? Why, you drunken fool, you! . . ." With some difficulty, he disengaged his hand from Mr. Glencannon's mustache and examined the palm of it perplexedly. "— Er — why, you're all sticky! Say — what in hell have you been drinking, anyway?"

"M'm, m'mp, varnish," mumbled Mr. Glencannon, detaching the fringes of his mustache from his lower lip and moving his jaws to get his teeth unstuck. "Aye — delicious auld vintage var-nish, whuch I remembered we had several gallons of, stored doon yonder in the forepeak. A-weel, as I was aboot to say, I was sitting there on an oil drum, sipping the varnish vurra genteelly oot o' a hole I'd punched in the tin, when all o' a sudden an inspi-ration struck me, *blosh!*, lik' that! Being a mon o' action, I. . . ."

"Oh, shut up, do!" said Mr. Montgomery dis-gustedly, turning his back on him. "— Yus, Com-mander Barry, I agree with you absolutely — we've got to keep on our toes. Them eighteen guards, plus the six Japs on the bridge, ain't something that a pack of 'arf-starved, unarmed coves like us can tangle up with bare-'anded!"

"Urg, but that's exoctly my point! If ye deduct. . . ."

"I know of two I'll damn well deduct," growled Captain Ball, looking toward the bridge. "Yes, and here are the two bare hands I'll deduct 'em with." He held them out in the moonlight, flexing the gnarled fingers and clamping them around a pair of imaginary throats. "Oh, I'll — I'll. . . ."

"Yes, of course, sir," said Barry. "But the thing we've got to look out for is the tommy guns. A man with one of those choppers is worth ten men without."

"— Whuch corresponds with my colculations exoctly," said Mr. Glencannon. "However, noo that we've got twelve o' those tommy guns oursel's, we. . . . "

"Lawks, good lawks, will yer listen to 'im rave!" groaned Mr. Montgomery. "Wot's the use of us trying to plan anything when that drunken idjit keeps on gassing?"

"Oh!" Mr. Glencannon stiffened. "Weel, noo, ye puling stirk, if ye dinna lik' my gassing, let's see ye do some gassing o' yere ain! For my part, urg!, I'm heartily tick and sired o' being scoffed and sneered. With the exception o' Captain John Ball, B.M.N., and Commander Thomas Barry, U.S.N., I think that the whole dom crowd o' ye are just so much urg!, and be domned if I'll speak to ye again, so there!"

"Welp, thank Gord for that!" said Mr. Montgomery fervently. "Now, maybe we can get somewhere with our plans. Yus, as Commander Barry 'as pointed out, tommy guns is tommy guns — and we mustn't forget the pistols that them skibby bridge officers carry, neither! Now, just as a suggestion, wot would yer think if. . . ."

"Now, wait, ker-hem, hold on a minute," Captain Ball broke in. "It seems to me like Mr. Glencannon has got something on his mind, and I wouldn't mind having him get it off it. Come, Mr. Glencannon — speak up and tell us what you was trying to tell us."

"M'mp! P'm!" said Mr. Glencannon, shaking his head and drumming his heels pettishly.

"Oh, his mouth's stuck shut again," said Captain Ball. He grasped Mr. Glencannon by the chin and forehead and opened him up on his hinges. "There, now — tell us your story."

Mr. Glencannon disengaged his tongue from the roof of his mouth. "Oh, vurra weel," he said thickly. "As I've been trying and trying to explain to ye, I was sitting doon there in the forepeak, quaffing the nectar off the top o' the varnish, when I chonced to notice one o' those big steel tubes o' fumigating gas that we used to kill the rats in the hold with after we'd carried grain cargoes. Weel, it occurred to me that if it wud work on rats, it wud work equally weel on Jops. So I sumply lugged it up into the starboard foc'sle, opened the door into the port foc'sle on a crack, stuck in the nozzle o' the bottle and turned on the gas."

"You did? — Wow!" Barry exclaimed. "How long ago did you do it, Colin? Quick, man — speak up!"

"Noo, dinna rush me, dinna rush me! There's still a guid ten minutes before the middle watch, and our lads in the foc'sle are all set with the tommy guns noo."

"You — you mean the Japs are dead?"

"A-weel, I doot if they'll ever be vurra much deader. Ye see, when I'd given the gas time to work, I held my breath lang enough to go in and open the portholes — and when the place had aired oot, we all went back and collected the guns. There was one for each Jop, and three extras, whuch mak's a roond dozen."

Barry looked at his watch and slid off the hatch to the deck. "Come on!" he whispered. "Let's go in there and organize things."

In the dim light of the forecastle, Hughes, the *Inchcliffe*'s bosun, was dealing out submachine guns to a crowd of seamen and firemen gathered around him.

"Okay — that does it!" said Barry. "Now listen, men; get this — here's what we'll do. Three of you stay inside here — one at each porthole and one at the door so you can cover the bridge. Everybody else hide a gun under his coat as well as he can. When the bell sounds for the change of the watch, go out on deck and head for your stations. I'll go last and follow you aft just far enough so I can turn around and get a clean shot at the two Japs on the fo'c's'le head. When you hear me fire, cut loose at every Jap you see." He took up a gun and walked to the door. "Three minutes more," he whispered. "Two minutes. . . . One minute. . . ."

Clang-clang! Clang-clang! Clang-clang! Clang-clang! went the bell. Barry drew a long breath and opened the door. "Okay," he whispered. Clumping over the high sill, the men filed out and started aft. Barry followed them, looking back over his shoulder at the Japs on the forecastle. At first he could see only their heads, silhouetted against the moonlit sky; then they moved to the ladder to await their relief. Barry wheeled, brought up his gun and squeezed out a burst of five. One Jap pitched headfirst to the deck; the other doubled over the rail and hung there, screaming. Simultaneously, the three men in the forecastle opened fire at the bridge and the battle was on.

It was an ugly, bloody and very horrible business. Four of the *Inchcliffe Castle*'s men were killed on the well deck in the first few seconds, but from then on it was the Japs who did the dying. The last one alive was Lieutenant Okimoto, and he had three bullets in his lungs. When he saw Captain Ball coming for him, dragging Lieutenant Nakagawa by the throat as though he were an empty sack, he climbed onto the dodger, thrust the muzzle of his pistol into his mouth and blew off the top of his head. He toppled backward into the sea. Still dragging Nakagawa's body, Captain Ball walked to the rail and peered down into the darkness; then, quite effortlessly, he heaved his burden overboard. "Shish-shish-shish to you, me lads!" he said, wiping his hands on the seat of his trousers.

It was getting light. The *Inchcliffe Castle* was headed for the mainland and the crew was busy with deck hoses and swabs.

"Anybody know where Glencannon is?" asked Barry.

"I 'aven't seen 'im since before the fight started," said Mr. Montgomery. "I shouldn't wonder if 'e's down in the engine room, ignoring the war where 'e left off."

"No, sor, he's in there in his room asleep," said Bos'n Hughes. "It appears that summat he et didn't agree with him."

Barry moved to the porthole and looked in at the figure on the bunk. The varnish had hardened in Mr. Glencannon's mustache and the bristles stuck out like porcupine quills as he mumbled in his sleep. "I am the Reverend Doctor Everett Hackthorne MacSnit, pastor o' the Feerst Presbyterian Kirk," he was saying. "I wonder if ye'd mind cashing a small pairsonal check for me?"

10

W ell, gentlemen," Admiral Sir Richard Keith-Frazer paused in his discourse and looked up and down the long teakwood table at the gathering of American, British, Australian and Dutch officers, "— Well, gentlemen — that, briefly, is the extraordinary situation prevailing on the Island of Kampan, as discovered and reported at such great personal hazard by Captain Ball, Commander Barry and this other gentleman." He turned and bowed to the trio seated at his right.

Not to be outdone in punctilio, Mr. Glencannon rose and returned the bow in a courtly manner. "I was only doing my duty, urp!" he said.

"Yes, yes, quite so," murmured the Admiral hastily. "Er — the task now confronting us, gentlemen, is to attack and reduce Kampan as soon as possible with the extremely limited surface and air forces at our disposal." He took a sip of water. "Since the *Inchcliffe Castle's* arrival with the news last week, the combined staffs have worked out what is believed to be a practicable method and have gone forward with the preparation of certain essential *matériel.* Commander Barry will now outline the general idea, following which we will explore the details and arrange the whole thing into a comprehensive formal combat plan. If you please, commander."

"Thank you, sir." Barry stood beside the sketch map of Kampan which was electrically projected on the wall. "Well, gentlemen, Admiral Keith-Frazer has described the Kampan setup very clearly. I believe you will agree that this narrow passage, here, is probably the key to the situation. Block that exit and the enemy is bottled up. . . . Recalling Hobson's exploit in sinking a collier in the mouth of Santiago Harbor in 1898, and the Royal Navy's brilliant use of concrete-filled block ships at Ostend and Zeebrugge in 1918, we propose to commence this operation by sinking such a ship crosswise in the channel, here." His upraised pencil cast a shadow on the map. "The vessel we have selected for this purpose is the Dutch freighter *Elzena,* five thousand, seven hundred tons. Her holds and most of her bunkers have been loaded with rock, which is now being pumped full of a mixture of sand and cement. When this hardens, the whole business will be locked into a solid mass of concrete." Around the table there was a nodding of heads and a murmur of approval.

"The big gamble will be whether or not we can get the *Elzena* into the channel — in other words, if we can fool the Japs into mistaking her for one of their captured ships running on their regular slave-and-booty route. Naturally, we are taking every precaution to make her look the part, even to having half a dozen Japanese-Americans on deck in case the picket boat comes close enough to hail us. But, of course, our main hope is the code — Secret Signal Code Number Four of the Imperial Nipponese Navy, which Admiral Keith-Frazer has already told you about."

"Urp!" said Mr. Glencannon, getting up and bowing again.

Barry glared at him. "But now I think we should consider a grave complication — perhaps I should say a great weakness — in the plan. I refer to the absolute radio silence which the *Elzena*, the aircraft carrier, the planes and the supporting surface units will have to observe at all times. Think, gentlemen, how this will hamper co-ordination, especially when approaching Kampan! At the most critical phase of the entire operation, when everything must synchronize to the second, we shall be without any means of inter-communication whatsoever!"

"Wah, hum!" yawned Mr. Glencannon, slumping down in his chair.

"Er, naturally, being a slow ship, the *Elzena* will leave this port well in advance of other units," Barry continued, frowning. "We will calculate her time of arrival at Kampan with the utmost care, for this will be the zero hour. Ideally, the bombers would attack at the very moment the passage is blocked. Actually, should they attack too soon, the enemy will attempt to get out his motor torpedo boats and his two cruisers. Should the bombing be delayed, he may blow up the block ship with depth charges, clear the channel and come out in time to destroy our comparatively weak task force. Any way you look at it, we're up against an extremely ticklish timing job. Well, sir — " he turned to the admiral "— the *Elzena* will be ready to sail at eight o'clock tomorrow night. I suggest that we now start working out a co-ordinated schedule on that basis."

"Right! Let's get busy, gentlemen! H'm, now let's see, figuring ten-point-three knots for the *Elzena*, we can determine a minimum running time of m'm, m'm. . . ." Admiral Keith-Frazer's pencil moved rapidly over the paper. Watching it, Mr. Glencannon's eyelids grew heavy, then heavier, and presently he slept.

He dreamed that he was a kilted lad again, back in the old Milngavie Reform School, releasing a matchboxful of bedbugs in the headmaster's chapel pew. Then, magically, the time shifted to the present and the chapel became Westminster Abbey, where

His Majesty the King was about to confer the Order of the Bath upon him before an audience of cheering thousands. He removed his kilt and was about to step into the tub when the King changed into the Queen, Westminster Abbey into New Scotland Yard and the audience into the entire London Metropolitan Police Force. The eighteen thousand constables drew their truncheons and started toward him menacingly. "Glencannon, will you come along with us?" they demanded with one voice — the voice of Commander Barry.

"Yes!" cried Mr. Glencannon, waking up with a jerk and staring around him wide-eyed.

"Okay — that gives us a chief engineer," said Barry, checking a list in his notebook. "You have shown your usual, er, commendable spirit, Mr. Glencannon." He coughed slightly to keep his face under control. "By the way, Admiral — as the enemy will undoubtedly start using radio as soon as we attack, it might be helpful if all these gentlemen had copies of that tattooed code."

"I agree with you, Commander. Mr. Glencannon, please report at Naval Intelligence Headquarters directly after lunch — they'll be expecting you. Well, gentlemen, I thank you. We stand adjourned until three o'clock."

As a matter of fact, it was only with the greatest difficulty that Mr. Glencannon could stand at all. Although the three days' diet of castor oil and enemas which he had recently undergone in the Royal Navy Hospital had blasted the last of the

varnish out of the nooks and crannies of his second-
ary plumbing, it had left him weak and shaky. And
now, of course, his nerves were completely unstrung.
"Ah, swith," Glencannon muttered, lurching toward
the door. "What frichtful, suicidal business has that
Yonkee boglie drogged me into noo?"

Emerging into the noontime bustle of Canberra
Street, he made for an establishment which bore a
sign, THE DOWN UNDER BAR. The place was
doing a rushing business and was filled with noise
and smoke, but he found a vacant table in a corner,
wilted down on the leather upholstered wall seat and
bade the waiter fetch him a double Duggan's. He
had had practically nothing to drink since before
breakfast and so, when the whisky arrived, he drank
it without the slightest hesitancy.

"So I'm sailing tomorrow nicht!" he croaked
miserably. "Sailing on a secret mission! A mission
to doom!" The words sounded like the titles of spy
films he had seen and this reminded him of his
imminent visit to Naval Intelligence Headquarters to
have his chest transcribed. He realized how deeply
he had become involved in dark and mysterious
transactions. "Ay, ye must be on yere guard, lad,"
he warned himself. "If any enema, er, enemy agent
knew aboot that code ye're wearing on yere buzzom,
yere life wudna be worth a pin's fee this minute!"
Drawing down his eyebrows, he glared from under
them at the drinkers lined up at the bar and seated
at the tables. Two or three were drunk and five or
six were so-so, but there was nothing about any of

them that would have aroused a layman's distrust. Mr. Glencannon, however, was not so gullible. "The ones that look drunk are merely clever actors hood-winking the sober ones," he decided. "On the other hond, those that are sober are plying the drunks with drink to mak' them drunker. Any way ye look at it, it's all vurra suspicious." With a masterly simulation of languid indifference, he sat back and toyed with his drink, occasionally bestirring himself to order replacements and to urp in a refined manner. To a casual observer, he was merely a gentleman of more or less distinction, whiling away a leisure hour by filling himself up with alcohol. Actually, of course, he was exerting his keen faculties to their utmost — looking, listening, studying the people around him. "Proctically every last one o' them is talking aboot the war!" he muttered. "Ho-ho, Glencannon, ye clever devil, ye've stoombled upon a vurritable nest o' spies! Weel, later on, when I have a moment to spare, I'll drap aroond to Intelligence Headquarters and turn in a full report on the place."

"— Er, pardon me, sir," a diffident voice came from the next table. "Did I understand you to say something about Intelligence Headquarters?"

Mr. Glencannon started violently, but at once regained control of himself. The speaker was, he saw, a pink-cheeked, white-haired old gentleman of comfortable build and benignant mien — in other words, a spy of the most deceptive and sinister type. He fixed him with a steely eye. "Oh, so ye've plonted a dictaphone on me, have ye?" he said, in tones as cold as ice.

"— A, er, dictaphone?" The other looked at him blankly. "I'm afraid I don't quite understand what you mean, sir. — It's only that when I heard you talking to yourself in a — forgive me — a rather loud voice about going to Intelligence Headquarters, I felt it my duty as a citizen to. . . ."

"Oh, ye did, did ye?" Mr. Glencannon broke in on him, taking the bull by the horns. "Weel, ye nozy auld enema agent — is it my fault if I'm hard o' hearing? Foosh!" He reached across and crashed his fist on the old gentleman's table. "If I didna realize that ye're far gone in yere cups, I'd arrest ye in the King's name this minute!"

"Oh, please, my dear sir!" The old gentleman quailed. "I — I'm an insurance agent, and I give you my solemn word I haven't been drinking! Look — I haven't even given my order! Come, sir — move over here and let's put an end to this unfortunate misunderstanding with a friendly drink! My name is Macklin," he raised his bowler hat politely, "— Robert Macklin."

A lesser man might have been caught off his guard, but not Mr. Glencannon. Obviously, he had been recognized; any attempt to deny his identity would be futile. The only course left open to him, therefore, was to pretend to be deceived by the fellow's protestations of innocence and play with him as a cat plays with a mouse. . . . He glanced behind him cautiously. "A-weel," he whispered, "it's a bit irregular for a secret intelligence agent to divulge his identity to a mere barroom scum, but just to be polite, I'll tell ye in strict confidence that my name is Glencannon and I'll tak' a dooble Duggan's."

"Yes, yes, by all means! We'll make it two!" beamed Mr. Macklin, vastly relieved. He summoned the waiter, then sat back and gazed upon his guest with the admiration and awe of a small boy beholding his first rhinoceros. "Well, well, well, Mr. Glencannon, I really can't begin to tell you what a pleasure it is to make your acquaintance! To one who has spent nearly forty humdrum years chained to an office desk, meeting a man of your adventurous calling is like a glimpse into another world!"

"Urp?" said Mr. Glencannon.

"Oh, absolutely! You, I suppose, have learned to take adventure in your stride — to walk through life in seven-league boots! And what a life it must be! Have you been long in the service, sir?"

"Since shortly after I was weaned," said Mr. Glencannon. "My feerst important case was running doon the notorious Mon in the Iron Mosk, but o' course my arrest o' Mata Hairy, the glomorous female lady spy o' World War One, is noo a chopter in history."

"— Mata? The beauteous, evil Mata? Ah, who hasn't heard of her?" breathed Mr. Macklin, rapturously. "— Wasn't she finally executed by a French firing squad at Vincennes?"

"Foosh, no!" Mr. Glencannon snorted. "Ye've been reading a lot o' cheap, troshy spy fiction! It's a matter o' record that I, pairsonally, gave her a guid, sound spanking, six smacks on each, and then burned her at the stake in the middle o' Piccadilly Circus."

"Br-rh! How grim!" Mr. Macklin shuddered. "But then, war is war — and, as the French themselves say, *que voulez-vous?*"

"I'll have another dooble Duggan's, thonk ye," said Mr. Glencannon. "— Then I shall proceed to entertain and thrill ye with a brief account o' my exploits ootwitting the Gestapo, the Ovra, the O.G.P.U. and the W.C.T.U."

As he talked, all signs of his earlier lethargy left him. He became dynamic, tense, alert; his brain was functioning with lightning speed and his whole plan of action unfolded crystal clear before him. Coolly, calmly, he would let this fellow ply him with drink and pretend to fall under its influence, and then! . . .

Tale followed tale and the afternoon wore on. The wily Macklin, feigning a slight befuddlement, tried to beg off accompanying him drink for drink. Mr. Glencannon would not hear of this, but the very attempt was damning, since it revealed the creature as a custodian of secrets so important that he dared not trust his own tongue! Thus, slowly, inexorably, the toils were drawing tighter.

"Aye, tighter than a tick!" said Mr. Glencannon. "— Er, haw-haw! Forgive me, auld mon — I was merely thinking aloud in code," he hastened to retrieve the slip. "Ye see, we in the trade have got our heads so full o' codes that it's a habit we soon fall into."

Mr. Macklin peered at him uncertainly through his gold-rimmed spectacles, which had slipped askew on his nose. "No, you don't really mean it, do you?" he asked, a trifle thickly. "Oh, come now — cut out the spoofing!"

"Eh?" Mr. Glencannon's brows beetled. He had been lying on so grand a scale for nearly four hours that to be challenged on this trivial point was an affront to his honor. "Eh? — Am I to understand that ye presume to doot my word, sir?"

"Tut, not at all, old boy! It's only that it didn't queem, er, seem quite plausible to me that any man should have so many colds in his head that he. . . ."

"Ho, so ye've got the audocity to sit there and call me a liar, do I?" roared Mr. Glencannon, rising to his feet. "Weel, ye sliddery auld glaggy, I've got codes all ower me! Look!" He tore open his shirt and fluffed up the nap on his chest.

Mr. Macklin leaned forward and viewed the tattooing in utter amazement. "— Good Lord!" he gasped "Why, this is the most extraordinary thing I ever heard of!"

"Oh, aye?" Mr. Glencannon chuckled sardonically and resumed his chair. "— Oh, aye?" In all modesty he could not but recognize that his action, though impulsive and seemingly indiscreet, had been a stroke of sheerest genius. For now, now he could drag this spy before any court martial in the British Empire and not only swear but swear truthfully that

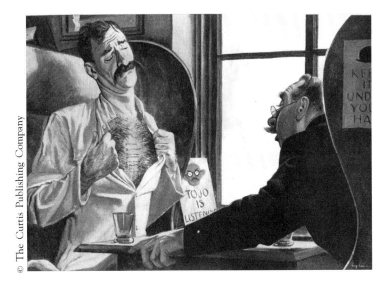

"Weel, ye sliddery auld glaggy, I've got codes all ower me! Look!" He tore open his shirt and fluffed up the nap on his chest.

he, Glencannon, had seen him, the spy, in the very urp, the act, of examining a secret military document with his, the spy's, own eyes! A few more such *coups* and he'd have the scoundrel in Piccadilly Circus, burning him at the stake!

Darting a quick glance at Macklin's countenance, he saw that it was turning green around the gills. The rest of it was definitely gray. . . . Now was the time to strike! Mr. Glencannon leaned across the table and smiled disarmingly. "Tell me, urp!" he asked in silken tones. "Did ye ever hear o' a secret Joponese base on the island o' Kampan?"

Macklin gulped before replying. "Why, no, I can't s-s-s . . ." His eyes went glassy and beads of sweat glistened on his forehead.

"— And did ye know that we're plonning to sink a block ship in Kampan Passage and attack the place within a week?" Mr. Glencannon pressed relentlessly.

The spy swayed dizzily and gripped the edge of the table. "M'm, wait — please, old boy — just a minute!" he begged, licking his lips and swallowing audibly. "*Bwah!* I — I know it's stupid of me to feel this way, but I'm afraid they've been coming a bit too fast for me, ha-ha! J-j-just ask the waiter to fetch me a raw egg in Worcestershire sauce, there's a good fellow. Good ole Mountain Oyster, see what I mean? Make a new man of me! Just lemme straighten up, and then you 'n' I can tell me all aboush ish! . . ."

It was nearly midnight. In Commander Barry's cabin on the lower bridge of the *Elzena*, he, Captain Ball, Mr. Montgomery and the three Australian officers who would accompany them were discussing the expedition. "Of course," Captain Ball was saying, "Mr. Montgomery and I made four trips to Kampan in the *Inchcliffe*, so I fancy we could take this ship in through the outer channel, even if the Japs spot us for what we are. Both of us took some rough bearings, just like you did, Commander, so perhaps. . . ."

There was a knock at the door. Mr. Montgomery unlocked it to admit Captain Kirkland, the chief district intelligence officer, who was wearing civilian clothes. He stood breathing hard and blinking in the light as he peered anxiously around the room. "Is Glencannon aboard?" he demanded bluntly.

"Why, no, sir! What's the matter?"

"All hell's the matter! He didn't show up at headquarters to have that code photographed, and now he's disappeared. Bob Macklin, our agent who was keeping him under observation, has disappeared with him." He spread his hands. "We've had the dragnet out since six o'clock, but so far there isn't so much as a trace."

For a moment there was stunned silence; then, "Whew!" said Barry softly. "That's bad."

"It's damned bad!" agreed Captain Kirkland. "— Gentlemen, it looks as though the Japs have got wind of this whole bloody show!"

"Whew!" said Barry, again.

11

All that night and the following day, the search went frantically on. No less than twenty-one private domiciles and eleven public premises were raided by government agents and the plain-clothes members of the civil police who were co-operating with them in the emergency. Thirty-six persons were brought in for questioning, but of these only three were held for further examination. One was an elderly suburbanite whose flower garden was found to contain a pile of fertilizer on which saltpeter had formed, thus making him criminally liable under "Par. VII, Sec. XIV of the Explosives Act of 1883 Relating To The Clandestine

Manufacture Or Storage Of Gunpowder Or Of Any Chemical Or Other Substance Or Material Susceptible Of Use As An Ingredient, Constituent Or Element Thereof." The other two prisoners were his daughters, one of whom had thrown a cake of soap at the arresting officers. As the young ladies happened to be identical twins and neither would admit the assault, there was nothing for it but to take them both into custody. Of Messrs. Glencannon and Macklin, however, the searchers could discover no trace.

The combined naval staffs had been summoned to a special meeting to discuss the situation. "— And so, as I say, gentlemen, it's almost as though the earth had opened and swallowed them up!" Captain Kirkland concluded his report.

"Ha-rumph! Well, at least you might find a more original way of saying it," Admiral Keith-Frazer told him grumpily. "Why are you so sure that the enemy is responsible for their disappearance?"

"Oh, it stands to reason, sir! Here in a city with a population of nearly a million, one man, and only one, is in possession of a secret Japanese code. That man is about to embark on an expedition to which the code is vital. Unknown to him, he is kept under constant surveillance by one of our most skillful agents, yet both he and his bodyguard vanish as completely as though the earth had opened and. . . ."

"Yes, yes — you've said that seven times already, dammit!" snapped the Admiral. "— What I want to know, Captain Kirkland, is why Intelligence didn't photograph that code before?"

"Because Glencannon was hospitalized as alcoholized, sir."

"Oh, H'mph!" The Admiral sat back, scowled at the ceiling and then recalled himself to the business in hand. "Well, gentlemen, we face a momentous decision; *shall we or shall we not proceed with the expedition as planned?* Before putting it to a vote, I think we ought to have Commander Barry's views, for his job is the basis of this whole operation. I needn't remind you that even with the code in his possession, the task which he volunteered to undertake would have been, er, fraught with peril. Without it, it is likely to be — if I may coin another phrase — a veritable suicide mission. — *A-hem!*" He shot a challenging glance in Captain Kirkland's direction. "— Well, Barry, I know you're not a tin hero of the sort that rushes out and gets himself blown to bits for a posthumous medal. I know you wouldn't risk your neck, your finger nail, or any other government property unless you felt the risk justified by at least some chance of achieving an objective. In other words, sir, you're not a bloody fool! — Well, Commander, the Kampan task force is assembled, instructed and ready. — What, in your judgement, should be the next move?"

"Sir," said Barry, "with your permission, the *Elzena* will sail at eight o'clock tonight."

And sail at eight she did, in inky darkness and a drizzle of rain. When she had groped cautiously down the channel through the blacked-out harbor traffic and under the spidery arch of the railway viaduct, the submarine guard net was opened for her and she took up behind the tiny, dancing light of the pilot boat which would lead her through the mine field.

Barry came out of the wheelhouse and joined Captain Ball in the starboard wing of the bridge. They stood in silence, sniffing the sea breeze that was dispelling the raw, dank smell of the concrete in the holds and gazing off at the loom of the lower town. The blackness, there, was relieved only by brief, pale beams of light as doors were quickly opened and closed and by sudden, brighter flickers which were followed for an instant by the glow of cigarettes.

"Well, here's hoping none of them buckos lights three on a match!" growled Captain Ball.

Barry nodded but said nothing. Mechanically, his fingers were tapping dots and dashes on the rail; they would hesitate for a moment and then go to tapping again. But gradually the signals became slower, then slower, and finally they stopped. Angrily, he thumped the rail with his fist.

Captain Ball stirred. "— It don't come back so easy, eh?"

"No, just parts of it. I'm only hoping I can remember enough so we can bluff our way through. But, damn it all, we shouldn't have to bluff! This thing's too important to depend on guesswork!" He pounded his fist on the rail again. "Look here,

Captain — What do you s'pose really happened to Glencannon?"

"Well, now, ker-hem, that's really a very mooty question. Ordinarily, I mean to say, I'd merely say that something he'd drank had made him drunk, and when Glencannon gets drunk, one thing is likely to lead to another. But it's that Secret Intelligence snooper disappearing along with him that I don't like the look of! His job was to keep tabs on Glencannon and if. . . ."

"Sh-h, wait a minute!" Barry gripped him by the arm and stood peering out into the darkness. "Did you hear a hail?"

"No!"

Barry glanced ahead at the light on the pilot boat. She was not signaling. "Funny!" he muttered. "I could've sworn I heard a voice. — Er, what were you saying, Captain?"

"Oh, yes, ker-hem! Why, I was just saying about that detective vanishing. As Captain Kirkland pointed out, it's almost as though the earth had opened and . . . Hark! Yes, yes — I hear it, now!" he leaned over the dodger and cupped his hands behind his ears. "— It's coming from dead ahead!"

"Yes! Listen! It isn't a hail — it's somebody singing!"

Somewhere in the gloom below them, a muffled voice was warbling an old Scottish ballad: *My Love Is Lik' A Red, Red Rose!* . . .

"*Glencannon!*" they gasped in unison.

They heard excited talk and the thud of running feet.

"You on the well deck!" Barry called, "What's going on down there?"

"There's somebody shut in the 'old, sir!" replied a voice. "'E's right under Number Two 'atch, singing like a lark!"

"Have it open, then! I'll be right down!"

While the tarpaulin was being unfastened and the wedges knocked out, the singing became increasingly louder. The ballad, now, was *Sweet Mary of Argyll* — a lovely thing! — and as the first plank was lifted off, it came welling up through the gap in a flood of melody which commingled deep pathos, unrequited love and 86.8 per cent grain alcohol.

Barry reached over the coaming and swept his flashlight across the rough concrete surface below. "Glencannon!" he called. "Where are you, Glencannon?"

The song quavered uncertainly, then subsided in a mumble.

"Where are you, Glencannon?" he repeated.

"Noo, wait a minute, let me think!" came a testy answer from the darkness. "— It's no' 'where are you,' but 'where art thou.' Aye, *Alice, Where art Thou?* Ho, I knew I cud recall it, if ye'd only shut up a minute!" There was a rapid glugging, as though liquid were being consumed from a bottle, and the sound of a throat being cleared. "There, noo — just start me off in the proper key, somebody, and I'll

sing *Alice Where Art Thou?* in a monner that'll bring
tears to yere eyes!"

A dozen flashlights darted in the direction of
the voice. Their beams focused upon a truly appall-
ing spectacle. There, buried up to his neck in the
hardened concrete and with only his right arm free,
was Mr. Glencannon. He had a bottle in his hand.
Beside him, also partially embedded, was an open
case of Duggan's Dew of Kirkintilloch.

"Quick! Bring some sledges and get him out
of there!" ordered Barry. "Of all the. . . ."

"Cripes! — Look!" came a horrified cry from
a sailor. In the trembling beam of his light, they saw
what appeared to be a severed head resting upright
on the concrete at the opposite side of the hold. It
wore a bowler hat and a pair of gold-rimmed spectacles that had slipped grotesquely askew on its nose.

"Well, my word!" said Captain Ball,
wonderingly. "It's almost as though the earth had
opened and swallowed 'em up!"

Barry swung himself between the planks and
dropped to the concrete below. He knelt beside the
head and removed the bowler. "He's alive, anyway,"
he announced. "Send for the doctor!"

"Look oot! Beware o' him, Tommy!" Mr.
Glencannon warned. "Feerst thing ye know, he'll
start plying ye with drink and. . . ."

Barry strode across and snatched the bottle
from Mr. Glencannon's hand. It was empty. "Come!"
he snapped. "Who is this other fellow, anyway?"

"He's a dangerous spy by the name o' alias Robert Macklin. I swore that sooner or later I'd trop him by hook or by crook, and ye can see how successfully I've succeeded!"

"Oh, so that's Macklin, eh? Well, good grief, I might have known it!" Barry emitted a thin sigh and rolled his eyes resignedly toward heaven. "All right, men — crack 'em loose and dig 'em up!" he ordered the sailors who were standing by with sledges and crow bars.

Macklin was the first to be exhumed. Doctor Ryan administered a hypodermic injection and shortly thereafter the patient opened his eyes. "Help!" he screamed, floundering around and thrashing his arms wildly. "I'm stuck! — I'm sinking! *I'm . . . sink . . . ing! . . .*"

"Sh-h! Take it easy — you're all right now!" the doctor soothed him. "How long have you been down here, anyway?"

Mr. Macklin lay frowning, as though striving to summon an elusive memory. Gradually, a look of anguish, of remorse, came over his face. He shuddered and closed his eyes. "I — we — we fell down here about twelve o'clock last night," he whispered. "The hatch was open, and Glencannon and I. . . ."

"Glencannon and you were drunk as coots — yes, yes, I get it!" said Barry grimly. "Well, my friend, at twelve o'clock tonight you'll be going ashore in the pilot boat — under arrest!"

"Aye, Robert Macklin, I arrest ye in the King's name!" thundered Mr. Glencannon, clambering up out of his hole. He drew himself erect and extended his right arm imperiously. There was a brittle, cracking sound, and all his clothing except the outstretched sleeve broke into fragments which fell clattering on the concrete.

For the next few days the *Elzena* hugged the coast on the first leg of her long and round-about voyage. She was making for the latitude along which she would run out to sea to a pre-determined position and there head straight down for Kampan Island on a course laid as from Pandalang. The weather was good and, considering the character of the mission, the spirits of all on board were astonishingly high. Now that Barry's worries about the code were ended, he was certain of success as he was of the sun and stars. He would sink the *Elzena* in Kampan Passage, and that would be that. He was fully aware of the awful finality implied by the words in their other sense, but he dismissed it from his mind. When bravery consists wholly in a lack of imagination, it is nothing but stupidity wearing brass buttons, and Barry's courage was not of that brand.

As for Mr. Glencannon, he was blithesome, gay and blooming as the rose. Scarcely an hour of the day went by without screams from victims of a hot foot, an exploding cigarette or some similar pleasantry, and life on board was gladdened by the sight and sound of him reeling about, slapping his thighs and guffawingly proclaiming himself the foremost wit of his times. On one occasion the engine-room staff

Scarcely an hour of the day went by without screams from victims of a hot foot.

contrived to introduce a handful of carefully collected toenail parings into his tobacco, but as they watched him smoking the blend with no reaction save a greater-than-usual relish, they realized what manner of man he was, and thenceforth gave up trying.

"I've never seen him in such fine fettle, blast me if I have!" Captain Ball remarked to Barry and Doctor Ryan as the three stood on the bridge watching Mr. Glencannon smear graphite grease on the deck outside the forecastle door. "If somebody'll just slip on that and break their neck now, you'll hear him laugh in a way that'll do your heart good!"

Barry frowned. "Oh, yeah? Well, if I didn't think his charming little whimsies helped to keep the men's minds off what's ahead of them, I'd put the damn hyena in irons."

"It's odd nobody's ever taken the trouble to murder him," observed the doctor thoughtfully. "— Still, I imagine it would need a bit of doing. Those twenty-two hours embedded in concrete jolly well ruined the other chap, but it worked on Glencannon like a therapeutic mud bath."

"Yes, to him it was a sort of Fountain of Youth, as you might say," Captain Ball agreed. "It simply blotted up all the old, stale alcohol out of him, so's he could start in afresh."

Later that afternoon they swung sharply away from the land and by nightfall were out of sight of it. This was the most dangerous leg of the voyage, since it lay straight across an area undoubtedly patrolled by the Japs to protect the flank of their Kampan Island route. For the next fourteen hours, or until the *Elzena* should actually be in the regular lane, no camouflage of Rising Suns, Japs on deck or use of secret codes could disguise her. Once sighted, her very position and course would betray her for what she was, and she would be sunk. Barry ordered the lookouts doubled and then asked himself why he had done so. Save for machine guns and small arms, the ship had nothing with which to defend herself. She was equipped for one thing and one thing only. But if something had to happen, he felt it would be better to see it coming. . . .

As the sun rose next morning, a long, faint wisp of smoke lay trailed across the horizon from a ship that had passed before dawn. "It's the first sign of traffic on Kampan Highway, gentlemen! Fifty minutes more and we'll be in the groove ourselves." Barry announced jubilantly. "We're running right on schedule, and. . . ."

"Submarine full on the starboard beam!" bawled the lookout aloft. "She's just surfacing about a mile away!"

Barry swung up his glasses in time to see the last white water cascade off her gray back as she came to stop and rested, pitching in the swell. Terns circled above her, perhaps mistaking her for a whale. "Break out the Japanese ensign aft and run up another one on the peak!" he ordered. "Get our Japs on deck where they'll show, and send Glencannon to me!"

He could see men in the sub's conning tower now, scanning the *Elzena* through glasses. A blinker commenced flashing. ". . . Identify . . . Identify!" he read. "Why, that's straight Japanese — They're not using code!" He trained the Aldis lamp upon her and answered, "*Elzena, prize, ex-Dutch. Pandalang to Kampan with prisoners and cement.*" There was a long, aching pause. One by one, a dozen little naked brown men emerged from the sub's forward hatch and went capering about the deck, limbering their arms and legs with calisthenics. Her blinker flickered again, "*Proceed.*"

Barry laughed nervously. "Whew!" He pushed back his cap and mopped the sweat from his forehead. "If those monkeys only knew what kind of cement we're taking to Kampan, they'd be tossing some fast ones into us with that deck gun."

Mr. Glencannon scowled through his binoculars. "Foosh!" he growled, scandalized. "The shameless gowks are fishing up buckets o' sea water and sloshing it on one another like so many schoolgirls. They're the fulthiest brutes in the world, Tommy, else why shud they always be taking baths?"

In a few minutes, the submarine vanished astern and the *Elzena* was alone again on the great blue, undulating plain. The dolphins streaked blazing beneath the surface, the flying fish skittered over it and the leaping mantas crashed down upon it with their mighty gray-brown wings. All this, everything — the sun, the sky, the clouds — was exactly as it had been, and yet a certain tenseness had come over the ship. For now they had seen the enemy — seen him, if not actually at home, at least near enough to it to feel greatly at his ease. Each tick of the chronometer, each turn of the propeller, was taking them nearer and nearer to as ugly a job as ever a ship's company would tackle.

In the middle of that afternoon, the lookout hailed again. "*Bridge, ahoy!* — A low, floating object dead ahead, maybe three miles!" he reported. "Looks like a lifeboat, but I can't make it out yet!"

"Keep your eye on it and report!" ordered the watch officer. "— You heard that, sir?"

"Yes," said Barry. "I wonder who except Japs could be fooling around in a lifeboat out here?"

"Maybe it's some prisoners who've escaped, like we was planning to do off of the *Inchcliffe*," said Captain Ball. "Aloft there!" he called. "What do you make of it now?"

"It's a lifeboat, all right, sir! I think I can see people in it!"

"M'm!" said Barry. "Well, Mr. Carter, we'll stop alongside of her to windward, please. Mr. Davis, post six men with guns along the starboard rail. If there are Japs in that boat and they're feeling their oats, let'em have it."

The little white craft was clearly visible now, and as she was swung by the swell, they saw a red cross on her side.

"Why, she's off a hospital ship!" Barry exclaimed. "Yes — there're people in her, all right! — Ring down to SLOW, Mr. Carter, and have a line ready."

As the *Elzena* slid alongside, he saw that four soldiers were lying unconscious in the lifeboat's bottom, while a fifth sprawled in the stern sheets, waving feebly. His khaki uniform hung in tatters, his long hair was matted across his eyes, and the rest of his face had been cooked into one great, angry blister by the sun.

"Stand by to receive a line!" Barry called. "Do you think you can grab it?"

"I'll try!" The voice was thin, piping. It was the voice of a girl.

"Hell!" Barry gasped.

The line was thrown. Stumbling over the thwarts, she managed to catch it and make it fast. "All right!" she called. "Take us aboard! Please hurry!"

Barry felt his knees go weak. "Captain Ball," he whispered. "My God, Captain, what're we going to do? We can't pick her up and — and simply take her to Kampan to be killed."

"No, we can't; you're absolutely right. Tell her you'll give her whatever she needs, but . . ." He shrugged helplessly.

Barry drew a long breath and leaned over the dodger. "Madam, I'm sorry, but I can't take you aboard. All I can do is load you with supplies and have my doctor give you all the medical aid possible in the next fifteen minutes. I can't delay any longer."

The girl sat down on a thwart and rocked slowly back and forth. "But you've got to take us aboard!" she cried. "These men are wounded — dying! They can't last another night in this boat!"

"I'm sorry, madam!"

She turned up her pitiful, blistered face and looked slowly from one to another of the solemn faces along the *Elzena*'s rail. "I don't understand," she said.

"Ker-hem, well, now wait a minute, Miss — I mean to say, look here!" Captain Ball intervened. "There's a war going on, see what I mean, and we've got military considerations to consider."

There was a long pause as the import of his words became clear to her. "Oh!" she nodded. "— Now I — I understand. —Yes, there's a war going on! Well, then, don't pick us up, if you feel you really shouldn't." She tried to smile. "We'll try to stick it out for a little while longer. But please, please send out a radio now, so that some other ship can find us quickly and. . . ."

"No radio message will be sent from this ship!" said Barry. He had to force himself to say it and it came out brutally harsh. He had often wondered if he would have the nerve to shoot himself and now, he knew.

The girl looked away. One of the wounded soldiers stirred and commenced singing *Waltzing Matilda*, beating time with a bandaged hand. She knelt to quiet him.

"Who are you, please, miss?" asked Captain Ball gently. "Maybe we'll be able to report you — later on."

Painfully, she dragged herself erect. "I am Second Lieutenant Florence Henderson, United States Army Nurse Corps, sir," she said. The effort was too much for her, and she slumped to the bottom of the boat.

Barry saw a white-uniformed figure shoot out in a curve from the deck below. It struck the water in a splashing belly-whopper, disappeared for an instant and rose to the surface, snorting. It was Mr. Glencannon. A few strokes brought him to the lifeboat. He grasped the hand line beneath the gunwale, dragged himself aboard and doffed his dripping cap.

"A vurra guid afternoon to ye, my dear Muss!" he panted, beaming most magnetically. "This is indeed a pleasure indeed!" He compressed his nostrils delicately between thumb and forefinger, leaned over the side of the boat and blew his nose into the water. "I am Muster Colin Glencannon, Esquire, fm'ff!" he introduced himself. "However, Flossie, ye may call me Colin, if ye'd rather."

The girl stared at him, wide-eyed, gave a piercing shriek and fainted dead away.

Barry reached over the rail and pointed a trembling finger at Mr. Glencannon. "You!" he snarled. "— Come back aboard this minute or I'll log you for mutiny and proceed without you!"

"Haw! Log and proceed and foosh to ye!" scoffed Mr. Glencannon. "Without what I've got on my chest, ye know how far ye'll get!"

"— What? Er? Oh!" Barry bit his lip and nodded slowly. He could hear himself breathing. He turned away from the rail. "Get that ladder down, Mr. Davis, and bring those people aboard!" he ordered gruffly. He had never felt so sad and so relieved in his life.

12

S o now you know what you're up against, Miss
Henderson, and goodness knows I tried to keep
you out of it!"

"Goodness knows you did, sir, but thank
goodness you didn't succeed!"

"Well, don't thank goodness, thank
Glencannon, if you insist upon thanking somebody,"
Barry growled. "If I were you, I wouldn't even start
feeling thankful — yet!"

"But my patients are still alive, sir!"

"— 'Still'! — Yes, and that's about the most
you can say for the poor guys!"

He didn't like this girl. She was one more
worry. She was a nuisance. In the fading light, the
thick layer of gray-green ointment on her blistered
face made her look like nothing human. She was
ghastly. Reluctantly, he had to admit that her eyes,
though bloodshot, were large and their lashes long
— that her hair, still matted with salt, grew down
to a graceful little peak on her forehead. Most of
all, he could not help noticing that she filled a
Japanese officer's uniform to vastly better advantage
than he had ever seen any uniform filled before. But
— he didn't like her. . . .

"Well, anyway, as soon as we get to the nar-
rowest point, I'll swing full left, like this," he continued, drawing a diagram in the air with the patient
impatience of the average man explaining almost
anything to the average woman. "That, as you see,
will put her crosswise in the channel with her nose
aground. Or do you see?"

"Yes, sir."

"M'mph! Well, right about then she may
start sinking under us. Maybe she'll have buckled,
if we've hit coral. Maybe the enemy's fire will have
holed her. In any case, the very instant she strikes,
I'll explode the charges in the engine room and blow
out both bilges, *Bang! Blooie!* She'll go down like
a rock!" He paused to get her reaction. There
wasn't any. He shrugged. "The bombers from the
carrier will start doing their stuff, the destroyers and
cruisers will close in behind us, and the transports
around on the other side of the island will be

debarking the American and Australian landing force. Oh, it'll be quite a show, for anybody left alive to see it — and with intelligence enough to appreciate it!"

"Yes, sir. — What about my patients?"

"— Pardon me? Oh, yes, by all means, your patients! Well, naturally, Lieutenant, an army officer of your high rank will understand that we've had several minor details to occupy us. Capturing Kampan, I mean, and destroying an enemy battleship and two cruisers, and releasing four thousand prisoners and — and a few little things like that. But of course, we hadn't forgotten such an important item as you and your four patients."

"Thank you, sir," she said.

He shot a quick look at her, but the mask of grease concealed whatever expression may have been on her face. Her eyes, though, had an angry glint in them.

"Yes, you and your four patients," he resumed coldly. "All of you will be conducted aft at the proper moment, by a competent naval officer. The wounded men will be lowered to a raft immediately after the explosion. You, lieutenant may either dive, jump, fall or get yourself shoved overboard, whichever best suits your military dignity. And from then on, you can either hope that the Japs don't snipe you before you get to shore, or hope that they do! Oh, and just for your information, all this will happen at approximately ten minutes past three o'clock tomorrow afternoon. — Er, are you looking for something, Glencannon?"

"Aye, Thomas, if ye'll pairdon the interruption. I left it up here a while agone, and — ah, here it is, here it is!" He reached under Lieutenant Henderson's deck chair, retrieved a whisky bottle and raised it against the evening star to gauge its contents. "Ah, swith, Muss — naughty, naughty!" He shook his finger admonishingly. "Ye've been helping yersel' to a wee drap on the sly!"

"No, sir!" Her tone was even.

"No? — Honor bright? Weel, it's just as weel!" he chuckled, tossing the bottle overboard. "Ye see, it really wasn't whusky at all, but a vurra obnauseous mess whuch I concocted oot o' engine oil and tobacco juice, and plonted here as a joke on the bos'n, who is one o' our stalwart Norwegian allies. I just noo saw two o' his stalwart Norwegian compatriots lugging him feet-feerst to sick bay, so I canna but conclude that my pronk was a howling success, haw, haw, haw!"

"Well, go and howl someplace else," said Barry. "I want to talk to Lieutenant Henderson."

"Weel, who doesn't?" said Mr. Glencannon, settling himself comfortably on the foot of her chair. "Noo, look here leftenant." He dragged another bottle from his pocket and thrust it under her grease-smeared nose. "I dinna ken what sort o' bellywash the ladies o' North America are accustomed to drinking, but Duggan's Dew o' Kirkintilloch is a superior and most exceptional product — the unvarying choice o' discriminating connoisseurs in clubs, bars, private homes and in fact wherever an aged, mellowed and truly select Scotch whusky is appreciated. Weel, then!" he removed the stopper and bowingly tendered her the bottle, "I invite ye to swill doon a guid, stout sowp o' it, with my cumpliments, and see if it doesna literally melt in yere mouth!"

"No thank you, sir," said Lieutenant Henderson.

"— Eh? No? Ah, losh! — Do ye really mean it? Come, come, then, Leftenant, let me offer ye a cigar!"

A snarling sound came from Barry's throat. He sprang to his feet and took a quick step toward Mr. Glencannon. Both men were surprised to find Lieutenant Henderson standing calmly between them. She turned her back to Barry.

"Mr. Glencannon," she said, extending her hand, "— Colin, I want you to know that I thank you from my heart for all your sympathy and kindness."

"— Eh? — Er!" . . . With rare presence of mind, Mr. Glencannon set the bottle carefully on the deck before crushing her hand between both of his own. "Weel, Flossie," he blushed modestly, "I am, as ye suggest, a vurra lovable character, and ye've got dom guid reason to know it! Ye're ugly as sin and yere pants are too tight, but ye can always count on my friendship, dearie!"

The sun came up and it was day — a day like any other. But it didn't feel so. There was something about it that tightened the stomach, parched the tongue, frayed the temper, took the kick out of the coffee and made the cigarettes taste like straw. Barry wondered if anyone else on board felt as rotten as he did. Yes, and as afraid! He had a hundred things to think about — things which, ordinarily, would have occupied his mind for hours. But now he seemed able to think of them all in the span of a second, and then his mind would dart ahead and dwell on matters of which it was foolish, fruitless and even dangerous to think at all. "Cut it out! Cut it!" he ordered himself savagely. "Keep your mind on your job. You're here to sink this ship in the channel, period. What happens to you from then on is none of your business!" It sounded fine, but it didn't work.

He went out on the bridge and joined Captain Ball, who was standing with his hands on the rail and his chin on his hands, staring moodily ahead. "R-r-rumpf! It's a hell of a note!" the old gentleman was grumbling to himself. "I mean to say, yes, yes, by gad, it is!"

"What is, captain?"

"*It* is! — To get to be my age and suddenly find out that you've got a yellow streak! Upon my word, if it wasn't for the flogging that them lice gave me aboard the *Inchcliffe*, I'd — I'd say let's chuck this whole show and turn around and go home."

"Well, I know how you feel, captain. To be perfectly frank, I'm not feeling so merry myself."

"No, and neither am I, thonk ye!" complained Mr. Glencannon, coming up the ladder. "For some reason, I keep tasting varnish. It must be some o' that stuff I dronk on the *Inchcliffe Castle*, because I've been on the wagon ever since, urp! — Weel, just as soon as we get home, I'll write a scathing letter to the monufacturers, just see if I don't!"

"When you get home? — What a hope!" Captain Ball laughed mirthlessly.

"Well, never mind that!" Barry hastened to change the subject. "Look here, Glencannon — I want you to stick around, and stick around close — understand? At any moment now, a plane may spot us, and I need you right here where I can read you."

He tried to sound brusque. Actually, he was sick with worry and weak with fear. Somewhere off to the southeast, he knew — or, rather, he hoped! — were the carrier and her destroyers. Away to the south, beyond Kampan, the transports and their escort were steaming, while to the west — perhaps even now swinging down to follow his own course — was the main striking force. All three of these converging elements would be keeping their planes aloft, to spot and shoot down any Jap patrols before they had time to give the warning — at least, that was the way it was supposed to work. . . . But in an operation of this magnitude so many things could happen! The Jap Hiro 97 patrol planes were old crates that could scarcely get out of their own way, but when he came to think of it, the catapult jobs from the cruisers weren't so hot, either. Well, suppose a Jap plane, just one, succeeded in getting a report through! . . .

"Look!" Captain Ball pointed at a cloud on the horizon ahead — a cloud that looked creamier than the rest, and somewhat darker underneath.

"Yes," said Barry simply, "that's it." He scanned the sky for planes. "Funny!" he muttered. "Can they be asleep at the switch?"

Gradually, the highest peak of Kampan thrust up over the rim of the sea, its head in the cloud. Away to port, so far off that she was hull down, a ship was plying northward. And presently a plane appeared. It was a Hiro, flying high. It held its altitude until it was directly overhead and then started down in a wide spiral, its throttled motors popping softly and sending out puffs of smoke.

"All right, Glencannon — you and I'll stand just inside the chartroom, where they can't see us. — Eddie!" he beckoned the Japanese-American signaler. "You handle the lamp — I'll tell you exactly what to send. Unbutton your jacket, Glencannon." He took up his glasses and trained them on the nose of the plane, waiting for the first flash. The great four-engined craft roared by at deck level, its crew waving to the *banzai*-ing Japs on the *Elzena*.

"She'll come around again and challenge us," said Captain Ball. But she didn't come around. Instead, she rose in a steep zoom, leveled off at a thousand feet and swung into a course due eastward.

"Well, I'll be damned!" Barry stared after her. "Are the monkeys getting careless or are we getting lucky?"

"Foosh! How can ye osk such a question, Thomas?" Mr. Glencannon demanded piously. "Dinna ye realize we've got an angel aboard — e'en though her yowp is blistered and she loathes yere vurra guts?"

"Well, by gosh, it looks as though we've got something plugging for us!" said Barry exultantly. "Bull luck, rabbit's feet or blistered angels, it's all the same to me!"

Mr. Glencannon looked shocked, but Captain Ball looked dubious. "Well, ker-hapf, I mean to say, I only hope the luck lasts! But there's many a sip twixt the cup and the lip, as the old proverb has it!"

"Ah, Captain, Captain, there's a world o' wisdom in those words!" sighed Mr. Glencannon, taking advantage of Barry's turned back to gulp a snort from a bottle which he quickly returned to concealment behind the chartroom door. "Still," he wiped his mustache with the back of his hand, "— still, if our luck holds only a little while langer, it will be lang enough. Look at yon island the noo!"

The lower peaks had become visible, although still but silhouettes. Barry looked at his watch, then moved to the chart table and took up the dividers. "We're ahead of time," he announced. "Mr. Murphy, call the engine room and have them slow her down five turns." He wished that, instead, he could order full speed and get there. Get there, get there, get there! Get it over with! . . .

Time dragged on. At noon, sandwiches and coffee were brought to the bridge, but were left untouched; indeed, scarcely a soul on board save Mr. Glencannon had any stomach for lunch, and even he confined himself to a few draughts of a simple liquid distilled from certain nourishing grains. But always, slowly, slowly, Kampan was rising out of the sea. It changed from gray to mauve, from mauve to green. The breeze bore the smell of jungle and forest and dark, damp earth. Barry's jaw muscles ached and the palms of his hands were clammy.

"That — that sort of shadow on the hillside there. . . . Isn't it the entrance to the passage?"

"Where?" asked Captain Ball. "Oh, yes, I can just make it out. Yes, that's it, all right. It leads down to the break in the surf."

"Bridge, there!" the lookout hailed. "A boat dead ahead, making for us! — Looks like an MTB!"

As Barry glanced at his watch, his hand was trembling. "Well, gentlemen, let's get set!" he said. He wondered if his voice was as strange to the others as it was to him. A whistle shrilled out a thin thread of sound. Orders were given in subdued voices. There was swift, quiet movement throughout the ship as all hands went to their stations.

The torpedo boat was coming fast, bucking over the swell and slapping out sheets of spray which dashed higher than her signal tripod. When she was still half a mile away, her blinker started flashing.

"All right, Glencannon!   Get set, Eddie!"
Barry was tense.   "Dot-dash-dash, dot-dot!" he read
the flashes and jotted them down on his pad.   "Dot-
dot-dash-dash, dot!   Good!   Er . . .   Damn it,
Glencannon!   Hell blast you, man — didn't I order
you to shave?"

"Aye, ye did, Thomas; ye did indeed!   But,
weel, ye see, I got thinking aboot the trogic fate o'
Samson and Delilah, and. . . ."

With a fearful oath, Barry snatched out his
pocket comb and thrust it into Mr. Glencannon's
hand.   "Here, you fool!   Get busy!   — Dash-da-da-
d-d . . ." Suddenly his voice failed him.   His mouth
hung open.   He leaned down and peered, wide-eyed,
wild-eyed, at the shaggy chest before him.   For the
code — the code — Secret Signal Code Number
Four of the Imperial Nipponese Navy — was gone!
Every last dot and dash, each tattooed numeral and
ideograph, had vanished as completely as the snows
of yesteryear!   Save for a random mole and a wen
or two, there was nothing!   Nothing!

Barry staggered back against the bulkhead and
grasped the edge of the door for support.   He struggled
to collect his thoughts.   Into his mind came the
words of Doctor Ryan: *"Those twenty-two hours embedded in concrete worked on Glencannon like a therapeutic mud bath."* . . .   Yes, that was it!   The cement,
the lime, the chemicals — something — had bleached
him!

"He's getting impatient, sir!"   The signaler
sounded nervous.

"Wait!" Barry stood with his hand over his eyes, trying to think. The day was Wednesday; therefore his first identifying signal should be either Six or Nine — but he couldn't remember which. The time was afternoon, so his second signal would be the word *zai*. *Zai?* No, *shin* — or, no, wait, wait! — shouldn't it be *han?* He was too upset to remember.

He uncovered his eyes in time to see the torpedo boat slow down and head parallel to the *Elzena*, perhaps three hundred yards away. Her blinker was flashing insistently and her three officers were scanning the ship through their glasses. His own signaler was looking at him questioningly.

"We have lost the code, Eddie." Barry spoke in Japanese, so as not to alarm the others on the bridge. "Send this straight: *Elzena, Prize, ex-Dutch, from Pandalang.*"

He watched the Japs as they read the signal, then saw them put down their glasses and discuss the situation. One of them made a quick gesture. Sailors went forward to the deck gun and trained it on the *Elzena's* bridge. *Stop!* spelled her blinker; *Your signals unsatisfactory. Send a boat. I will board you.*

"Like hell you will!" Barry sprang from the chartroom into the wheelhouse. He grasped the telegraph handle, shoved it to FULL AHEAD and shouldered the helmsman away from the wheel. He crowded on full right rudder. "I'll ram the monkeys!" he shouted. "Murphy, tell the engine room to sock it to 'er! I'll show those sons of. . . ."

SHROOF! A shell ripped through the overhead.

"Fire! Come on! What are you waiting for?"
Barry yelled.

From all over the ship, rifles cracked and
machine guns stuttered. The water around the torpedo boat leaped up in little white geysers. Her deck
gun flashed again. There was an ear-splitting WHAM,
a stunning shock as the shell struck the end of the
Elzena's bridge. The window in front of Barry was
covered with blood. "Start that wiper going!" he
ordered. "— No! No, shut it off — it only smears
it! Wind the glass down, Quartermaster!"

The torpedo boat darted ahead. Her motion
made her deck gun useless, but she opened up with
a pair of heavy machine guns. Barry cursed as he
saw that there wasn't a chance in a million of ram-
ming her. Well, if he hadn't been born an utter
fool, he would have seen it in the first place! In
another minute she would be in position to launch
her torpedoes, and then. . . .

"What a mess, what a mess!" he groaned.
The sound of bullets hammering on the wheelhouse
was head-filling, deafening. It was like being inside
a giant bass drum. Black pocks rose on the white
bulkheads as the paint flaked off the dented steel.
Then suddenly the noise was stilled and the black
pocks ceased appearing. The torpedo boat commenced zigzagging wildly, the water all around her
spouting and seething under a hail of tracer bullets
that streaked out of the sky. Howling like sirens, six

planes dived past the *Elzena* and bore down upon the other craft with all their guns blazing. As they flashed by, Barry saw the White Star insignia. They were American! Higher up, there were dozens and scores of them — the entire carrier group!

"By gad, Barry — they're early!" Captain Ball panted, joining him at the wheel. His cap was missing and his forehead was covered with blood. "Ha! That's done it! They've snaffled her! My word, just look at 'er!" The little craft was belching flame from end to end; even the surface of the water around her blazed with the escaping gasoline. All at once there was a bellow as of thunder as her torpedoes exploded, and that portion of the sea in which she floated shot up into the air in a majestic white column which stood shimmering in the sunshine for a long second and then collapsed upon itself in a cloud of mist.

"*Nippon banzai!*" screamed Barry, shaking his fist at the white patch of seethe where the boat had been. "Shish-shish-shish! So Sorry!"

"Sorra?" Mr. Glencannon stood unsteadily in the doorway. "No, no, dear lad, ye've really no cause to apologize to me. Ye were a wee bit hasty, that was all. As I was aboot to explain when ye lost yere temper, Samson and Delilah, and also Esau, who was vurra hairy also, also all had vurra . . ."

"Shut up!" snapped Barry, putting the ship back on the course. He glanced at the sky over Kampan. It was speckled with black puffs of anti-aircraft shells and streaked with long, white vapor trails left behind by the dive bombers as they peeled off and hurtled down. A continuous thudding rumble rolled over the water.

"Ker-hem, I mean to say, they're giving 'em hell!" grinned Captain Ball, wiping the blood from his face. "Er, look, Barry — I think you'd better just ease her over a little more to port. — Easy, Easy — there, that does it! If you'll head for that black rock, right there where the waves are shooting up, we'll be fine for the next five min. . . ."

S-S-SHROOF-F-F! S-S-SHROOO! Shells plunged into the water on either side of the *Elzena.* Instinctively, Barry bore down on the wheel, intending to zigzag, but Captain Ball restrained him. "No, don't — the channel's too narrow," he warned. "You've got to hold her exactly as she bears." He looked up at the green mass looming ahead, searching for the battery that was firing upon them. He saw a flash in the trees, then a puff of smoke. It was followed in quick succession by three more flashes; then, suddenly, an area of perhaps an acre was sinking with multiple flashes and smoking like a volcano.

"Why, by George — they're under fire themselves!" he exclaimed.

"Aye, there's six o' our destroyers and a cruiser aboot three miles astern o' us," said Mr. Glencannon.

"What?" Barry relinquished the wheel to Captain Ball, stepped out onto the bridge and looked aft. Yes, there they were, sure enough — dodging in and out of the smoke screen with bones in their teeth and guns blazing. "Oh, my God!" he groaned. "The whole timetable has gone cockeyed!"

Just as he re-entered the wheelhouse there was a blinding flash, a sickening explosion on the forward well deck. Through a cloud of smoke he saw the mast topple slowly to starboard, smash the bulwarks and slide into the water. It hung dragging by its shrouds, pounding the side of the ship, and then tore loose. Most of the deck had been blown away; the derrick booms and a tangle of wreckage lay on the concrete below.

He felt the ship go out of control and start taking a sheer. Turning, he saw Captain Ball slumped down on the matting.

A quartermaster sprang to the wheel, but Barry waved him away. "No, I'll take her! Get the doctor!"

Shells were falling all around them now. Six float zeros came roaring from astern and raked them with machine guns. One of them belched black smoke, yawed crazily and plunged into the sea directly in the *Elzena's* path. The ship swam over it as though it were a leaf.

Barry, now, was standing at the wheel with his shoulders hunched, his eyes alternately on his landmarks and scanning the water around him. He saw the familiar masses of weed and sea tangle surging back and forth on the submerged rocks and heard the booming of the surf even above the thudding crash of bombs and guns. Then the surf sound dwindled; the ship was in the calm patch. Now was the time to swing her. He turned the wheel, she came slowly around, and there, open before her, was the canyon — Kampan Passage. The far end of it was blocked with smoke that was drifting from the lake. The *Elzena* could run in unnoticed, at least by surface craft.

"Well, we've finally got a break!" said Barry. Nobody answered. He glanced back over his shoulder. The quartermaster, Mr. Murphy and two seamen were lying dead on the matting. Mr. Glencannon sat with his back against the bulkhead. Lt. Florence Henderson, her white uniform spattered with red, was kneeling before him, tying off an artery in a gaping wound in his leg.

Barry squared his jaw and jammed the ship as closely as he dared to the right-hand side of the passage. She scraped a rock for three quarters of her length, shuddering and screeching as her plates caved in. But the narrow stretch — the key to Kampan — lay just ahead. She couldn't sink until she got there. She couldn't! She couldn't!

He sounded a blast on the whistle — the signal for all hands below to abandon stations. He moved his hand toward the switch that would touch off the scuttling charges.

Suddenly, plunging out of the smoke ahead, came the gray bulk of a cruiser. Sheets of white water were curving from under her bows and a great ragged fragment of her camouflage netting still streamed from her foretop, lashing out behind her like the hair of a witch in the wind.

Two of her forward guns blazed simultaneously.
. . . It seemed to Barry that he, the *Elzena* and all
of Kampan Island had been struck by lightning. He
was paralyzed. He was blind.

"Glencannon!" he called. "Glencannon!"

His sight came back to him. It was dim, but
he could see the cruiser. She was still coming! Fast!

"Glencannon!"

"Aye!" The voice was close beside him.

"Colin! Take the wheel! Swing her over!
Swing her over! Quick!"

"Aye!"

The *Elzena* slewed broadside in the channel.
Her nose crashed into the rocks on the far side. Just
as the cruiser struck her amidships, Barry closed the
switch.

There was a roar like the end of the world.

By noon of the following day, the battle had
died down to desultory rifle and mortar fire in the
hills as the last of the Japs were consigned to their
ancestors. Clouds of greasy black smoke still billowed up from the blasted carcass of the battleship
Hoshino, while at the center of the lake a cruiser
floated bottom upwards. The water around her was
dotted with white birds too heavy with food to fly.
The second cruiser was part of a shapeless, piled-up
mass of concrete, steel and scrap iron that blocked
Kampan Passage.

"My God!" Admiral Sir Richard Keith-Frazer
murmured in awe as his barge drew in alongside the

tangled heap that yesterday had been two ships. "My God! *Dulce et decorum est pro patria mori.* . . ." He removed his cap and held it across his breast as he stood in contemplation of the fearful spectacle. In the cockpit behind him, the officers of his staff made similar reverence.

All that remained of the *Elzena* — at least, all that could be distinguished of her — was her bow, her bridge and the jagged stump of her funnel. The port wing of the bridge was twisted down into the water. The bowman of the barge engaged his boat hook around an awning stanchion.

"Gentlemen," said Admiral Keith-Frazer solemnly, "I think I should go aboard her for a moment." He leaned over, grasped the *Elzena*'s rail and straddled across the gap. Slowly, laboriously, he made his way up the steep, bloodstained slant to the blackened wreck of the wheelhouse. He paused for a moment to catch his breath, steadying himself against the edge of the doorway, and then stepped within. After the brilliant light of the tropic noon, the interior was dark. And the Admiral's eyes were old.

"Good day, sir!" came a voice — the voice of a girl.

"Eh?" The admiral took a groping step forward. "Who's that?"

"Second Lieutenant Florence Henderson, United State Army Nurse Corps. I regret that I cannot stand up to salute you, sir."

"Eh?" The admiral passed his hand over his eyes. Slowly, slowly, things took form, then color, then detail. He saw bodies. Then he saw the girl. She was sitting on the deck with her back wedged in a corner. She was wearing a blood-spattered Japanese uniform. Her hair was matted and her face horribly blistered.

"Why — my dear!" The admiral knelt beside her, "My dear!" It was not until then that he saw a man stretched out with his head pillowed on her lap. With an effort, he recognized the face as Barry's. "Oh, my dear! Are you — is he — I mean? . . ."

Barry's lips fluttered. His eyes opened and he smiled. "We're okay, sir. You can ask the Lieutenant!"

The admiral turned to the girl and raised his eyebrows questioningly.

"You heard what the Commander said, sir," she answered. "I — I — guess we're okay!"

"Ker-hem! I mean to say, bless you, my children!" came a benevolent voice from the opposite corner.

"Ah, foosh!" came another voice from somewhere.

MR. GLENCANNON IGNORES THE WAR